Munozm
Munoz Molina, Antonio
In her absence

in
ABSENCE

in her
ABSENCE

ANTONIO MUÑOZ MOLINA

Translated from the Spanish by
ESTHER ALLEN

Other Press • New York

This work has been published with a subsidy from the Directorate-General of Books, Archives and Libraries of the Spanish Ministry of Culture.

Originally published as *En Ausencia de Blanca*, by Antonio Muñoz Molina.

Production Editor: Robert D. Hack

Text design: Kaoru Tamura
This book was set in ACaslon by Alpha Graphics of Pittsfield, NH.

10 9 8 7 6 5 4 3 2 1

Library of Congress Cataloging-in-Publication Data

Muñoz Molina, Antonio.
   [En ausencia de Blanca. English]
   In her absence / Antonio Muñoz Molina ; translated by Esther Allen.
      p. cm.
   ISBN-13: 978-1-59051-253-1
   ISBN-10: 1-59051-253-7
   I. Allen, Esther, 1962-   II. Title.
   PQ6663.U4795E6313 2006
   578.77'89—dc22

                                        2006038139

in her
ABSENCE

One

THE WOMAN WHO was not Blanca came down the hall toward Mario wearing Blanca's green silk blouse, Blanca's jeans, and Blanca's ballet flats, her eyes narrowing into a smile as she reached him—eyes the same color and shape as Blanca's, but not Blanca's eyes. She welcomed him home in a tone so identical to Blanca's that it was almost as if she really were Blanca, and she stooped a little to kiss him because she was slightly taller than he was, just like Blanca. But instead of the daily absentminded brush of her closed lips against his, she opened her mouth to Mario's tongue, and he, startled by this unanticipated ardor, didn't respond in time.

In the warmth of her breath and the brief, carnal softness of her lips he felt as if he'd gone back in time to Blanca's first delicious kisses, now identical, but falsified with a flawless or almost flawless precision that made everything all the more unreal. He was grateful for the touch of those long, soft hands even though they weren't Blanca's hands, the odd way she had of putting her arm around his waist as she led him toward the dining room, as if he, its owner, didn't know his way around the apartment where he'd been living for some time before he met Blanca, or as if the apartment, too, were a precise replica of something that had been lost: the apartment, the pictures in the hallway, the dining room furniture that Blanca objected to, and rightly so—when Mario bought it he'd had pitifully bad taste—the tablecloth embroidered by Mario's mother or grand-mother, the dishes, the steaming bowls of a soup just cooked by the impostor or near-double of Blanca who'd taken it off the stove and served it when she looked out from the balcony and saw Mario crossing the street toward the apartment building. (But Blanca, the real Blanca, the one from before, might never have looked out from the balcony to see if he were coming.) The soup smelled better than ever, Mario thought almost remorsefully, noticing for the first time not that he was beginning to give in, but that the possi-bility of giving in existed, comprehending with melancholy and relief that he wouldn't be able to keep up this suspicious hostility, uncompromising vigilance, and desperate solitude forever. Unlike Blanca, the woman now sitting across from him didn't dab her lips with the corner of her napkin after each spoonful, didn't raise her eyes in silent reproach if he made the slightest noise as he ate his soup, and didn't sit motionless without say-ing a word until he realized it was time for him to bring the tray with the main course and fresh plates and silverware on it from the kitchen.

Blanca would never have lit a cigarette before clearing the table, much less settled down on the sofa to watch TV without first straightening up the dining room and cleaning the kitchen until it was spotless. In fact, Blanca hardly ever watched TV, nothing but the news and a strange late-night program with jumpy images and a heavy-metal sound track called *Metropolis*, which once ran a piece about the painter she'd just broken up with when she met Mario. Sure of herself and fraudulent, dressed in Blanca's own clothes—the silk blouse that had almost exactly the same feel as her skin, the jeans so tight they made her seem taller and more curvaceous—the woman who was not Blanca leaned back on a wide black leather pillow and watched television, her feet now bare, Blanca's flats lying on the floor next to the sofa. She was smoking a cigarette or rather just holding it, having forgotten it so completely that if Mario, with deft and steady fingers, hadn't taken it from her just in time she would have burned herself or spilled ashes all over the rug, perhaps damaging it. Wary, always on the lookout for signs of imposture, Mario studied her feet that, though often a little the worse for wear, were long and delicate with a faint blue tracery of veins in the instep. This time he was surprised to see no sign of chafing or roughness on the heels and as his eyes moved further he discovered that the toenails were adorned with red polish, something he'd never seen on Blanca's toes before. But then immediately he wondered about that. It wasn't the kind of thing he'd ordinarily notice; Blanca herself had sometimes complained that he paid no attention to the clothes she wore or the new touches (nothing too ambitious; they didn't have much money) by which she tried to improve the apartment's somewhat rudimentary decor. Yet he really did think—yes, he was sure—that Blanca had never polished her toenails. But even as he strained his memory to achieve clear certainty he began to doubt and despair, finding, all the while, that Blanca's shiny red toenails and softer and smoother feet were very delectable. He remembered the night before, how she'd wrapped her arms around him from behind after he switched off the bedroom light, warming her cold feet against his legs with a physical complicity that would have been gratifying if it weren't for the obvious imposture, the fact, more bitter now than astonishing, that this woman, so identical to Blanca, was not Blanca, could not be Blanca.

She seemed to be dozing off while Mario cleared the table, but then opened her eyes and held them steadily on him at a moment when he was watching her from the kitchen. He realized that nowadays it was only when she wasn't looking at him that he dared scrutinize her intently, out of a superstitious wariness that was quite futile and frequently embarrassing, for this Blanca-like woman always caught him at it immediately, was always smiling at him in weary tolerance. Right now, for instance, as he washed the dishes, he'd been watching her from the kitchen, trying to see whether her chest was rising and falling, thinking he could make out the placid rhythm of her breathing against the babble of the soap opera, beginning to grow bolder. Little by little, without realizing it, still clutching a damp dishtowel, he'd moved toward the dining room door, stepping out of the corner of the kitchen where she couldn't see him with a ridiculous mixture of caution and recklessness. With every step he took, his face was undoubtedly taking on the particular expression of a person who's watching someone else in the belief that he himself is unobserved. Just then she opened her eyes, with no trace of surprise, and of course no alarm, as if she'd heard his footsteps or had been able to tell, from the sound of his breathing, that he was approaching. He was never sure whether he would actually find Blanca there the next minute or what her mood would be: Blanca could intuit everything about him without needing to open her eyes, but lately that secure knowledge of him no longer seemed to be slipping into disdain or the unthinking, perilous neglect of a woman who's grown used to taking her lover's loyalty for granted.

The eyes from which Blanca did not look out at him lingered for a moment on the damp dish-cloth he was still holding, then rose to meet his own evasive gaze and held it. Blanca's hazel eyes, Blanca's straight black hair, her faintly freckled nose, the dark pink of her lips, Blanca's own rings on the same fingers where she wore them, her wedding ring, which he would have liked to examine more closely to see whether the forgery had been so painstaking that this ring, too, was engraved with the date they met rather than the date of their wedding, because both agreed (though the idea originated with Blanca) that what deserves to be remembered isn't the official ceremony but the first meeting, with its rare mixture of chance and destiny.

Mario went closer and watched her curl up small on the sofa and then stretch out her arms in pleasurable indolence, her hair hanging loose now, her face sleepy and ready to nod off, her blouse almost entirely unbuttoned, the silky fabric of her bra on view, the sweet cleft between the breasts that seemed so much like Blanca's breasts, though he no longer knew for sure whether their shape and the pinkness of the nipples was or was not identical to the breasts he remembered. He heard her saying his name in Blanca's voice, almost more tender now than ever before, without the faint note of cool distance whose existence he had always refused to accept, just as he had refused to see and understand so many things, so many slight untruths, so much silent disloyalty. He took one more step, put the dishcloth down on the table, afraid his hands still smelled of grease or detergent, and knelt down next to the sofa, next to the woman whose breath carried nuances different than Blanca's yearned-for breath or the succulent taste of Blanca's mouth. As he leaned toward her, he was surprised by a renewed excitement, an unexpected liberation from nostalgia, if not from suspicion. It occurred to him that he, too, was learning how to pretend, and he tried to justify this by telling himself, as he pushed the hair away from her face and kissed her eyelids and nibbled an earlobe perhaps slightly fleshier than Blanca's earlobe, that this apprenticeship in simulation would help him root out the lie—and not simply in order to make his peace with it, never that. But the fact is that as he kissed and caressed her and unbuttoned her green silk shirt all the way down, he closed his eyes very tightly so that there would be moments when he was sure he really was kissing and caressing Blanca, recognizing her in that willed darkness with a certainty neither his intelligence nor his emotions could grant him.

Two

MARIO LÓPEZ ALMOST never went out for a beer after work with his colleagues. He wasn't in any way unsociable and prided himself on getting along well with everyone in the office, but each day at ten minutes to three when the staff left the Provincial Council building and dispersed in eager, noisy groups to various nearby bars, he always invented some excuse or simply waved an energetic good-bye and quickened his steps to get home as soon as possible so that he could open the door and call out to Blanca by no later than five past three or, at the very most, ten past.

The only greed he could conceive of was greed for time spent with her. If he yielded seven hours of his life each day to the civil service, and devoted seven more to sleep, any carelessness in the use of the ten hours that remained for living with Blanca would be a reprehensible squandering, a quotidian amputation of happiness. He had never lost the avid and perpetually unsated need to be with her that he'd first experienced during their early days, when they'd spend an afternoon together or go out to dinner and then not see each other again for a week or two, when he didn't yet dare call her every day from fear of seeming too pushy.

Their years of marriage hadn't diminished his amazement at having her regularly there beside him, for hours and days and weeks and months, a greater wealth of time than he'd ever dreamed of possessing and that might have lasted so long because it could turn out to be inexhaustible. Sometimes all he needed to do was open the door of their apartment to be welcomed by the familiar signs of their domestic life and Blanca's habitual and ever-desirable presence: the smell of something cooking in the kitchen, the sound of Blanca putting plates and silverware on the table, maybe even the theme song that accompanied the opening credits of the afternoon soap opera—but that was only on days when he was exceptionally quick and got home at three o'clock sharp, days when there were no last-minute snags at the office or annoying encounters in the street. Other days, he would open the door and hear nothing, smell nothing, and for a fraction of a second, standing just inside the front door with his keys in his hand, he'd be overwhelmed by a devastating, entirely unfounded panic: Blanca had been obliged to leave very suddenly without having time to let him know, to be with her mother in some health emergency; Blanca had been in an accident; Blanca had left him. But this would last only a second or two: he'd call out to her and hear her voice responding from the far side of the apartment or from behind the closed door of the bathroom, or else the explanation was simply that she was so distracted in her studio, so immersed in a book or classical radio program, that she hadn't heard his key in the lock. He would hear her footsteps, then see her coming down the hall toward him, and he would feel as if Blanca were coming back from somewhere very far away, from a secret cellar or crypt whose existence he was unaware of and where he would never be allowed to follow her. He felt the same way sometimes when he phoned her from work in the morning. After only three or four rings Mario would already be jittery with fear that she wasn't there; then he'd hear her voice and it was the voice of someone who is alone, lost in thoughts or rooms that no one else knows anything about. When she read a book, listened to music, or watched a movie, Blanca had a marvelous ability to sink deep into herself and disappear entirely from the external world. This absolute concentration was something Mario had learned not to interfere with, the proof of a sensibility that was a constant wonder to him but made him feel dull by comparison. Sometimes he felt intimately deserted, wanting to tell Blanca something or ask her a question but knowing it wasn't worth trying, not because she'd pay no attention but because she literally was not there; she'd taken leave of her senses, as people used to say, in the most literal meaning of the words, taken leave of the reality that so often bored or disgusted her.

His fellow workers poked fun at Mario for his big hurry to get home. Either Blanca had him on a very tight leash indeed, they speculated, or else the two of them absolutely couldn't be apart from each other and were still behaving like newlyweds even after several years of marriage. The latter theory secretly made Mario very proud, for he considered it to be true; however, out of an almost religious compunction and sense of reserve, he didn't join in the jokes and sexual allusions the suggestion inspired in his colleagues. His life with Blanca was too precious to be intruded on by anyone's humorous comments, not even a close friend's—though in point of fact he did not have any close friends. The crude sexual innuendo heard around the office when no women were present or, worse still, in his male colleagues' bar conversations after work, reminded Mario of barracks talk. Its brutality was always directed against women, especially against the one who mattered most to him, his wife.

This was another of the reasons he rarely went along for a beer after work. He'd sit there in silence, unable to take any interest in the other men's tales of adultery, and this was sometimes rather awkward. He didn't join in the ritual complaints about married life, he was no good at telling jokes, cigarette smoke bothered him, beer and political arguments made him sick to his stomach, he was bored. At times when he had no choice but to participate in the group's celebrations—before Christmas, or when one of the higher-ups had a birthday and invited everyone out for drinks and tapas—he'd spend the whole time glancing surreptitiously at his watch and trying to laugh almost as boisterously as the others; he strained to hear stories he had absolutely no interest in and off-color jokes that were already stale when he was a teenager, and when he decided that a prudent amount of time had passed and he'd drunk a couple of beers or glasses of wine, he'd invent an urgent pretext and leave, but never without some office wit making the customary jocular comment about his rush to get home—to punch in his time card, they'd tell him, even more punctually than he did at the office.

Mario didn't care. He breathed the outside air in relief and walked home with light and happy footsteps, even though he was exhausted and felt as if he'd expended all his energy fighting off some sticky, clinging organism. What a waste of time it was not to be always with her, to have her nearby and be able to look at her, even if she was immersed in her own tasks; what an unbearable desert the job and the Council and life in the city of Jaén would be if she didn't exist, or if she hadn't fallen in love with Mario and, against all expectation, decided to marry him, in one of those sudden impulses that were the most attractive aspect of her character and also, at times, the most fearsome.

Blanca would often say they led a life from which great experiences were absent. He conceded that she was right, but also thought, on his best days when he'd get home a few minutes before three after a workday devoid of annoyances, that for him there could be no greater experience than simply walking home along the same route as always in the knowledge that unlike all the other men he went by in the street—men drinking in bars and talking about soccer with cigarettes in their mouths, men with hungering faces pivoting to watch a woman walk past—he alone had the privilege of desiring beyond all other women the precise woman he had married, and the absolute certainty that when he opened the door of his house, he would find her there.

It was true that they did live in Jaén—not exactly the center of the universe where cultural activities were concerned—and that neither of them had a particularly exciting job and Blanca quite often had no job at all. But these limitations mattered less to Mario than he himself said they did, and in any case they were more than made up for by a set of fortunate circumstances that, as he saw things, it would be idiotic to disdain. They had a good apartment, on the eighth floor with a balcony overlooking one of the city's main boulevards, purchased by Mario at an excellent price before the real estate fever of the 1980s. During a time of financial uncertainty and economic crisis, Mario had secured a permanent position with the civil service, with a salary that, while not exactly substantial, always saw them through the end of the month, and a work schedule, from 8 a.m. to 3 p.m., that allowed him to do other jobs in the afternoon, though he didn't much like having to leave the house. He sometimes considered enrolling in the university: he was a draftsman but hadn't given up on the idea of becoming an architect—or rather Blanca hadn't given up on it. Actually, the career that most appealed to him was being a quantity surveyor or, as they're called nowadays in Spain, a technical architect—the term Blanca preferred. Sometimes when they were with her friends, Blanca was a little vague about her husband's line of work. She skirted around the word draftsman, but the term she absolutely could not bear to utter was bureaucrat. When talking about the sort of people she most detested, people who were ruled by habit, monotonous people devoid of all imagination, she'd say "They're mental bureaucrats."

It didn't take much of this kind of talk before Mario López began to wonder sadly whether he himself had been categorized as a vile mental bureaucrat, and whether Blanca might not be including him in the crowd of people who were vulgar, bourgeois, and as tedious as the routines of their workdays and marriages.

Days before one such comment, on a Monday in June, he got home at two minutes after three, precisely twelve minutes after clocking out of the office. During his habitual walk home he'd been enjoying the day's salty, almost maritime breeze, with a whiff of coming rain that was exceptional for that dry city at that time of year, a breeze that rattled the canvas awnings and made you feel like living life to the full. As he opened the front door, he took in the ordinary household smells with elation and gratitude: cleanliness, freshly waxed furniture, the food Blanca had just finished cooking for him.

Six years after meeting her he was still moved each time he reentered her presence. As he was calling to her for the second time he saw her coming toward him from the back of the apartment. He knew immediately that she was in a good mood and would offer him her mouth when they kissed, which wasn't always the case. He set his briefcase down on the ground to give her a hug, and looking at her lovely face, now so near, he remembered one of their rare fights. Blanca, unthinkingly, in the heat of an argument he, too, had done his share to provoke, an argument that cost him weeks of regret and stubborn resentment, had accused him of settling for too little, of lacking, she'd said, "the slightest ambition." Whereupon Mario had suddenly grown very calm and answered that she, Blanca, was his greatest ambition, and that when he was with her he wouldn't and couldn't feel the slightest ambition for anything more. She looked at him very seriously, tilting her head to one side. Then her eyes filled up with tears and they fell into each other's arms and onto the sofa, kissing and gasping for breath as they groped for skin beneath clothing, trying not to hear the television trumpeting the theme song of the nightly news.

Three

NOW AGAIN THE news was on as they started their lunch. Mario had come home so early that the news wasn't over yet. He was savoring the vichyssoise, one of Blanca's best dishes, and as he did so she stopped and looked at him, her spoon suspended next to her mouth in a gesture of condescension or censure, he wasn't sure which. He was afraid he might have slurped and ate the next spoonful with great care, pressing his lips together in silence, swallowing discreetly, and immediately wiping his mouth with the edge of the napkin.

Blanca had impeccable table manners. She always sat up very straight, taking the napkin from her lap and laying it on the table before she stood up. There was a perfection in her way of peeling an orange or persimmon with a knife and fork that to Mario, a former altar boy, had an almost liturgical quality and reawakened his old social inferiority complex. Mario peeled oranges with his hand, sinking his thumbnail into the peel, and when he really liked a sauce or a salad dressing he had to make an effort not to sop it up with a bit of bread.

He remembered perfectly the first time in his life he'd ever tried to eat with a knife and fork, which was also the first time he learned that the two were used together. (In his parents' house they always ate with a spoon, and they picked up the pieces of rabbit that accompanied their rice on Sundays with their hands.) It was in the cafeteria of the old Jaén bus station, on a trip he and his father had taken from their village for some medical or bureaucratic reason. To the child who was Mario, Jaén was terrifying; it stank of danger and sickness and the dank office where hostile officials made him and his father wait—and when his father, normally such a forceful man, spoke to the officials, he lowered his voice and bent his head toward the floor. He and his father were sitting on stools at the cafeteria's counter and were served a combination platter that struck Mario as the height of luxury: two fried eggs with potatoes and a pork chop on the side. He tore off a piece of bread with his hands and dipped it in the egg, then set about eating the meat the same way he always ate strips of bacon for lunch in the country: laying it out on the bread and then cutting it with the knife. But his father told him that they were in a fine restaurant in the province's capital city; he should take a look around and watch how everyone else was eating their meal—with a knife and fork. If Mario insisted on staying in school, his father added with a note of sarcasm, he might well want to start behaving in a more refined way and imitating the table manners of the gentry. Mario, who'd always been quick to blush, felt his own ludicrousness burning in his face as, beneath his father's mocking eyes and the sidelong scrutiny of the customer sitting next to them, he tried to figure out which hand was supposed to hold the fork and which the knife. He didn't succeed in cutting off a single bite of the pork chop, and when he finally managed to spear a bit of egg with the fork and tried to lift it to his mouth he ended up staining the good pants his mother dressed him in on Sundays and the holy days of obligation, and for trips.

What a meager life I'd lived, he thought, if the cafeteria of the Jaén bus station struck me as a luxurious dining establishment. He'd tell Blanca about these things and she would laugh, but he didn't know if she was touched by the thought of Mario's primitive past, so different from her own childhood, or simply astounded by the existence of this picturesque way of life that was fundamentally absurd to any civilized person who took an interest in its peculiarities. The odd part of it, given her class background and the little she knew about the real life of people who were poor and working-class, was that Blanca's political leanings were much farther to the left than his own. In 1986, the referendum on Spain's entry into NATO had triggered one of the few truly bitter fights they'd ever had. Mario thought that a yes vote was both prudent and reasonable, while Blanca wore a pin bearing a large NO, collected signatures, attended meetings, and participated in demonstrations alongside people whose politics Mario considered loathsome: leftist extremists who were simultaneously in favor of pacifist disarmament and the terrorist attacks in northern Spain. When he saw how sad and dejected she was on the night of the vote, Mario couldn't rejoice at the fact that his side had won. He felt guilty and even a little reactionary.

As he ate his vichyssoise, Blanca had begun explaining something to Mario about a cultural project in which she might be offered some sort of minor role—as a translator, perhaps, or a costume designer—but he wasn't paying much attention, though he pretended to be absorbed in what she was saying. What really interested him, what was keeping him absorbed, weren't Blanca's vague hopes for employment, which so often came to nothing, but her daily, miraculous presence, the slightly nasal sound of her voice, the way she moved her lips, the focused and serious attention with which her eyes rested on him as she told him about someone apparently very famous who had just arrived in the city and whom they would both very soon have the chance to meet in person. The name, Lluís Onésimo, seemed familiar to Mario but he didn't want to ask anything more about the man for fear of seeming ignorant. Also, he'd just heard something from the television that had completely distracted him, or rather put him on guard.

The anchorman was talking about a Frida Kahlo exhibition that had just opened in Madrid. When she'd seen the show advertised in the newspaper the day before, Blanca had fervently resolved that they must go: this was a unique retrospective, a once-in-a-lifetime opportunity. With sorrow and remorse, he'd reminded her that it was nearly the end of the month and there wasn't enough left in their budget to cover the cost of the trip, the hotel, and the restaurants in Madrid. The show would undoubtedly stay up for several months, he told her by way of appeasement, though he knew it was futile. Anyway, they'd do better to wait until summer vacation; this was the busiest time of year at his office and what he really felt like doing when he got home Friday afternoon was staying home and relaxing, not setting off on an exhausting trip to Madrid and coming back on Sunday night by the express train that got into Jaén at 7:00 Monday morning, which meant, as he knew from past experience, that he'd have to go directly from the station to the office without even time for a shower.

Blanca said nothing, lowered her head, and went to her room and shut the door as soon as they'd finished eating and cleared off the table. Nevertheless, her face didn't look terribly serious; she had only a faraway air of disappointment that

Mario had learned to recognize in a slight fold that formed at one side of her mouth when she gave him a perfunctory smile, out of politeness or as a gesture of kindness, or not even that, as a sign to him to leave her alone: it wasn't something worth arguing over or even talking about.

Guilty, ashamed, afraid of losing her, Mario knocked softly on the door. When he heard only music from the radio, he opened it cautiously and saw that Blanca was stretched out on the sofa in the dark, in the small, warm room that was her place of refuge, even though it looked out on an airshaft crisscrossed with clotheslines and the neighbors' voices, noisy television sets and shouting children that were always audible in there and kept her from concentrating. She had an old writing desk, a gift from her mother, with little drawers that she kept locked but that he often wished he could open. Blanca's pens and pencils were always lined up on top of it, inkwells with sepia-colored inks, the notebooks where she jotted down thoughts, copied down poems and phrases, pasted clippings from magazines and newspapers, the lilac-tinted stationery and envelopes with her name printed on them, her name, which made Mario happy just to see it written out.

He sat down next to her on the edge of the sofa and ran his hand over her smooth, straight hair, over her cheeks that were wet with silent weeping. He begged her pardon, blamed himself for being such an egotist, and told her that if she wanted, they'd go to Madrid that very weekend. Blanca asked him in a low voice to please leave her alone, and she begged his forgiveness as well, blaming herself for being depressed and frazzled: it was the terrible heat that was already starting to set in, the ever-problematic first day of her period. She stood up, her hair disheveled, and Mario thought in sorrow and fear that she had the same empty, drawn look on her face as during the early days, when he was already in love with her without being able to imagine that Blanca might some day pay him sufficient attention even to take full note of his presence, much less reciprocate his feelings.

Twenty-four hours later, when he thought the crisis had passed, Mario, his back to the television, silently savoring a spoonful of exquisite vichyssoise, watched Blanca's face, waiting for the signs of enthusiasm and subsequent glumness that the name Frida Kahlo would inspire there. She'd see one of Kahlo's paintings on the screen, one of the self-portraits Mario secretly considered abominable, and she'd regret not living in Madrid and not having the time or money to travel wherever she wanted. She'd probably even stop eating, or stop speaking to him, withdrawing into silence as if into a room that would forever be inaccessible to him, writing for hours on end in one of the notebooks she kept under lock and key.

The name Frida Kahlo was repeated two or three times more, and each time Mario feared Blanca's inevitable reaction, like someone who sees a flash of lightning and waits, counting the seconds, for the thunder to come. But the announcer moved on to developments in the world of sports and Blanca was still talking to him about a possible job; he couldn't really understand what it involved but encouraged her warmly to pursue it. If only he'd paid a bit more attention, if only his obsessive vigilance hadn't betrayed him by keeping him from observing this new danger, the new name that was beginning to crop up in her conversation.

He thought, without being able to acknowledge the thought to himself, that what Blanca really needed was to spend some time studying and then take a civil service exam that would lead to a steady job. If she could devote herself to an ongoing, tangible enterprise, it would take her out of her daydreams or at least offer her a solid anchorage in reality. Maybe the fact that she'd paid no attention to the news about the Frida Kahlo exhibit was a good sign; perhaps she was about to change, but not too much, only a little, just enough to stop withdrawing so frequently into silence, and stop rejecting the idea of having a child with such cutting hostility. "I don't think we have the right to bring anyone else into this horrible world," she'd say.

Another man might have thought she was flighty, but for Mario Blanca's endless sequence of new and different jobs and widely disparate enthusiasms was proof of her vitality, her audacity, her innate rebelliousness, qualities he found particularly admirable because he was largely devoid of them. By means of bitter struggle and scholarships that were always meager, he'd come to Jaén from his village, Cabra de Santocristo, to complete high school, surviving the sad winters of the end of childhood in boardinghouses, and graduating with excellent grades in days when there were still tough exams to pass in order to qualify for graduation. Then, frightened by the length and difficulty of the training period for a technical architect—the career he would have chosen—he'd become a draftsman. Six years younger than he, born into another social class and raised during the days of color television, yogurt, and annual vacations at the beach, Blanca had a far less punitive idea of the world. No one had ever inculcated into her the two principles that loomed over the childhood of every male of Mario's generation and peasant class: that he was born into a vale of tears and that he had to earn his bread by the sweat of his brow.

Blanca came from an opulent Málaga family of lawyers, notaries, and land registrars, but she'd never wanted to benefit from these social advantages. Mario thought this was heroic, although he disapproved of her frequent and vehement mockery of all her relatives, beginning with her mother, a menacing widow who wore false eyelashes, smoked Winston Super Longs, and never paid the slightest attention to anything except herself—but who had, more than once, helped them out of a tight spot with an overnight bank transfer or a check made out to cash.

Penury makes people fearful and conformist; it's the secure possession of money, Mario suspected, that awakens and nourishes audacity. He enjoyed reading works of contemporary history and had noticed that most if not all revolutionary leaders were not of working-class origin. The occasional financial help from her mother aside—and between those occasions whole years could go by—Blanca lived off Mario's salary and her sporadic earnings as a hostess at conventions, a translator of catalogs, and, eventually, an exhibition guard, but she'd grown up in such great economic security, her sense of entitlement was so innate, that she never felt any fear about the future, and never bothered to behave prudently in view of future benefits, to the extent that both times she'd had a formal contract for a full-time job, she quit after only a few months: the daily routine exhausted her or she couldn't stand dealing with a boss who was making passes at her. For a person with a temperament like hers, Mario told himself, a day job was worse than a prison sentence.

Her nonconformity and impatience had also propelled her into enrolling for and subsequently abandoning two different university degrees, one in fine arts and the other in English philology. Unlike most people her age, Blanca, who was about to turn thirty, had renounced nothing: she wanted to paint, she wanted to write, she wanted to know everything there was to know about Italian opera or Kabuki theater or classic Hollywood movies, she wanted to travel to the most exotic cities, the most imaginary countries, her eyes would grow moist watching *Lady of Shanghai* or listening to Jessye Norman, and she'd read aloud in tones of throbbing excitement the reviews in the *El País* Sunday supplement that extolled the gastronomic delights on offer in the great restaurants of Madrid and San Sebastián, delights that, since they had Italian or French, if not Basque names, Mario was unable to imagine. Each time they ate in a restaurant, he would turn out to have forgotten the names of the different varieties of pasta and the French culinary vocabulary she'd tried to teach him, and it was now a classic joke between them that he'd never be able to remember what *gnocchi* meant, or *pesto* or *carpaccio* or *magret de canard*, not to mention the even more inaccessible terminology of the Asian cuisines, for which Blanca developed such enthusiasm during a certain period that she learned to use chopsticks with the same ease and precision as she handled a fish knife, until finally the lack of any good Chinese, Japanese, or Indian restaurant in Jaén discouraged her.

When they went out to dinner with friends of Blanca's, all of them experts in wine and gastronomy, Mario very gladly put Blanca in charge of ordering for him, but Blanca didn't make jokes about her husband's culinary ignorance in front of other people and would even attribute preferences to him he hadn't known he had, and that sounded like flattery: "What Mario really likes is a good fondue," or "Mario doesn't trust the sushi they serve in that Japanese place in Granada."

Mario defined himself as the type who ate to live rather than lived to eat, but that didn't keep him from appreciating and being grateful for Blanca's culinary subtleties. The things she cooked had a smoother and more delicate flavor, with strange hints of sweetness or acidity that were always a little bit surprising, and even unexpected shades of color as nuanced as their aromas and flavors. He loved the way Blanca cooked as unconditionally as he loved the sound of her voice or the way she dressed; still, he wasn't sure that her presence wasn't the principal condiment of dishes that might otherwise have been rejected by his rustic palate, educated or irreparably desensitized by the noodle soups, beans, garbanzos and lentils, tough meat and potatoes, and truly lamentable fish served at the boarding house.

The flavor of the meals she cooked filled him with a sensory emotion that was similar to the effect of her kisses: it was the feeling of the new, all that didn't belong to him, that was unknown and inaccessible, all the things he would never have known existed were it not for Blanca's presence and influence. Money, he thought, doesn't only educate you, it also gives a particular sun-kissed glow to your skin and frees you from fear of uncertainty; money makes you cosmopolitan, teaches you to use foreign languages and foreign eating utensils, to feel at home and at ease among strangers. He, who was never sure which hand should use the fish fork, was overwhelmed by admiration when he saw Blanca's speedy and dexterous handling of her chopsticks in Chinese restaurants; she could pick up a few grains of rice or a small, lustrous bit of lacquered duck with infallible precision.

If he enumerated, one by one, all the characteristic things about her that he recognized and treasured, Mario couldn't think of a single one that didn't have a kind of meticulous, secret polish of perfection and spontaneity. His love was watchful and serene in equal measure: he loved her as much for the color of her hair as for her radical political convictions (however extreme he sometimes found them), as much for her sexual attractions as for the exquisite way she had of peeling an orange or pronouncing a sentence in English, and the scent of her perfume was as important to him as the intellectual level of her conversation. Little by little, he was even managing to like almost all Blanca's friends, especially the gay men from whom he had nothing to fear. The one he didn't like in the slightest from the very beginning, even before meeting him, from the ill-fated moment when he heard his name spoken for the first time, was the individual called Lluís Onésimo, dramaturge or dramatist or something like that, multimedia artist, hypnotizer, con man, *metteur en scène*, as Onésimo would say, gazing at Blanca as if Mario didn't exist, speaking French in a thick Catalán accent and sprinkling his conversation with terms that very soon echoed through Blanca's and her friends' vocabulary: *stage, Mediterranean, virtual, installation, performance, mestizaje, multimedia.* Words like these instantly aroused an instinctive hatred in Mario; they were as virulent as a gob of poison spit or the quick, lethal sting of a scorpion—and what made it even worse was that only he, Mario, had been hit with the gob of spit; the sting was lethal only to him.

Four

OF COURSE ONÉSIMO was neither the first
moth drawn to the flame of Blanca's intellectual
charms nor the first parasite to feed off her unconditional reverence for any form of talent or skill.
Blanca tended to squander her admiration like a
foolishly generous heiress frittering away her for-
tune among swindlers and freeloaders. Except for
Mario, whose only remotely artistic skill was line
drawing, all her former boyfriends and almost all

her current friends were practitioners of one art form or another and were voraciously interested in all forms of artistic expression without exception, including bullfighting, hairdressing, and Spanish pop music. It was the 1980s, and in the mysterious hierarchies of the day, tailors, hairstylists, and flamenco-ish singers were worshiped with the same reverence as painters and sculptors. At first this surprised Mario, who'd been raised with the almost fearful respect that the poor have for art and knowledge, but he gradually came to find it natural, and not only because a person can always get used to anything. As it turned out, after he'd taken a closer look at the works of the painters and sculptors Blanca frequented, he couldn't find much more merit in them than in a haircut.

His instinctive caution and lacerating inferiority complex kept him from expressing opinions such as this one. What often happened as well was that he had absolutely no opinion at all but was forced to improvise one for fear of looking stupid. He was afraid of saying something wrong or offensive, but more than anything else he was afraid of demonstrating that he wasn't at the intellectual level of Blanca's friends.

Her first boyfriend when she was a teenager had been a fledgling singer-songwriter almost as young as she was. She ran into him again many years later, well after marrying Mario, during a Week of Singers and Their Songs that the government of the region of Andalucía was sponsoring in Jaén. When they went backstage to say hello after a performance he'd secretly found pitiful, Mario was initially a little jealous of the way Blanca hugged her former love, but he started calming down when he saw that the teenage hero she often reminisced about was now a guy with a receding hairline that his anachronistic ponytail did nothing to conceal. The popping buttons of his tight shirt, its shoulders liberally sprinkled with dandruff, further enhanced his general air of bewilderment and poor hygiene. The singer told them about a record with lyrics by Jaén poets that the Provincial Council's cultural department was going to produce for him, and about a possible tour through Nicaragua and Cuba. Blanca never mentioned him again, and Mario struck his name from the imaginary list of potential enemies.

The next few chapters of Blanca's sentimental biography involved a photographer, a would-be film director, and a professor ten years her senior with a passion for Puccini. Like the successive strata of an archeological excavation, the cultural enthusiasms she clung to long after leaving the lovers who first instilled them in her were what remained to bear witness to the history of her heart: Cartier-Bresson, *Turandot*, Eric Rohmer. The arts of painting and sculpture had come into her life relatively late in the day. When she met Mario, she was still suffering from the final repercussions of an all-consuming and disastrous relationship with the painter Jaime Naranjo, also known among the more up-to-the-minute or obnoxious of his unconditional adherents as Jimmy N.: the *enfant terrible* of the local avant-garde who routinely carried off all the province's official prizes.

Mario had noticed that the previous decade of Blanca's love life was a lot like the lives of the women whose biographies she collected: Misia Sert, Alma Mahler, Lou Andreas von Salomé. She was even thinking of writing a very long essay about Salomé, and early drafts of it filled some of the notebooks that were carefully aligned on her desk. First in Málaga and Granada, then in Jaén, Blanca had had passionate relationships—though some of them on a purely intellectual level—with men whose erudition and intelligence gave Mario a secret inferiority complex when he heard her talk about them. She'd inspired their desire, but not only that: also songs, poems, paintings, and even, people said, a certain novel that had met with considerable success. She owned its manuscript, personally dedicated to her by the author, and kept it among her own books in a special corner over her work table alongside other manuscripts, volumes of poetry, screenplays, short story collections, and even sheet music, all with inscriptions to her by their authors.

On the living room walls were drawings and engravings signed and dedicated to her, and a poem handwritten in red, green, and yellow ink by the legendary Rafael Alberti—to whom Blanca, who'd spoken to him half a dozen times, referred simply as "Rafael." In the bedroom, over the headboard, hung a large semiabstract canvas by Naranjo, painted shortly before his breakup with Blanca, and on the opposite wall was a nebulous, yellowing engraving by Fernando Zóbel that had the considerable virtue of putting Mario to sleep. His response to art was often physical, sometimes almost to the point of an allergic reaction: Frida Kahlo, for example, made the roof of his mouth feel as if it were coated with grease, and Antoni Tàpies (fortunately not an object of Blanca's devotion) inspired a mixture of weary sorrow and heartburn. He forced himself to feign interest nevertheless, and reproached himself bitterly for his lack of sensibility, the random paucity of his reading, the private lethargy and pent-up resistance he often harbored when accompanying her to a concert, a movie, the premiere of a new play, or an art opening where everyone knew everyone else and greeted Blanca effusively and the paintings looked like doodles or tiny insects and all the young people of both genders were uniformly dressed in black and afflicted with a ghostly pallor. Often on such occasions Mario would get the terrifying feeling that he was caught in a trap he would never break out of, a situation that would never end: experimental jazz concerts where the musicians seemed to be wringing out their instruments and the notes lasted for hours that were eternities; art openings with endless rounds of greetings, kisses on both cheeks (between men, even), glasses of lukewarm champagne, ecstatic congratulations, and meaningless gossip; dance performances in which a single musical phrase or given electronic rhythm was repeated ad infinitum and without the slightest variation.

There was never any opera in Jaén, to Mario's great relief, but once, during one of their exhausting cultural pilgrimages to Madrid (they had to see everything, make the most of every minute of the weekend), Blanca took him to a contemporary opera in a theater that had once been a local cinema, on a beautiful, lively plaza in Lavapiés where Mario would have liked to sit, have a beer, and watch the people go by. But he didn't dare say so to Blanca, and of course he didn't like the idea of letting her go into the theater by herself at all. The composer of the opera in question was an individual she'd met in Granada who had introduced her to electronic music and the twelve-tone scale and who had phoned her personally to invite her to the premiere, catapulting her into transports of joy and impatience. When he said hello to her in the lobby of the theater (which was called—to Mario's greater anxiety—the Center for New Theatrical Tendencies), the composer leaned forward and shamelessly planted a kiss on her mouth while giving her ass a squeeze with his big hairy hands. Even so, what he most resembled, Mario thought, was a Quaker preacher, dressed all in black and not wearing a tie, with a heavy beard but no moustache. But the worst of the ordeal was the opera itself: seemingly devoid of beginning, end, plot, or order, it went on and on, mercilessly, eternally, and just when it seemed about to conclude it would start up again. When it was finally over, Mario—defeated, demolished, and with a throbbing headache—cast a surreptitious glance at his watch while hypocritically joining in the audience's applause and saw to his amazement that this infinite torture had lasted a mere two hours.

Luckily, Jaén was not known for the dynamism of its cultural life. Whole weeks could go by, especially during the summer, without any special event that absolutely couldn't be missed. But it was during those periods that Blanca's melancholy longing to travel grew most acute; she'd study the cultural pages of all the newspapers and want to go to Madrid, Salzburg, or even nearby, privileged, almost mythical Granada, where it seemed that the life of the mind never took a rest, where all movies came out right away, some of them in the original, undubbed version, and where there were perpetual international festivals of every variety, including classical music, jazz, theater, even tango.

Around that time, Blanca had developed a taste for the boleros and tangos that were starting to be played in some of the bars they went to on weekends, granting Mario the relief of a midpoint between the symphonic boredom of the concert halls and the industrial-strength heart-monitor noise of the nightclubs, where the music, if it can really be called that, was even more unbearable than the shouted conversations, cheap liquor, and cigarette smoke.

For Blanca's twenty-ninth birthday, Mario had prepared a modest surprise: two cassettes of boleros by Moncho that were so rare they didn't seem to figure in any catalog of the singer's work. He'd spotted them by chance on the counter of a gas station. As he listened to a particularly sentimental bolero in the car on the way home, he felt, from his stomach to his chest and throat and then up into his tear ducts, a dense wave of inexplicable anguish and irrevocable happiness, a happiness that was like a memory of happiness, reaffirmed and exalted by the passage of time. Alone in the car, waiting for the light to change at a fountain commemorating battles long past, his heart melted and his eyes filled with tears, and his pleasure was not only in his love for Blanca, but also in this absolute proof that he could enjoy, without the slightest uncertainty, an aesthetic emotion previously enjoyed by her, certified by her.

How many times in his life had he tortured himself over a painting, a movie, a piece of chamber music, wondering whether he really liked it, whether he'd look stupid if he moved his head in time to the music or tapped his foot on the floor, and whether the next break in the music would be the end, requiring immediate applause, or only a short pause, one of those moments of silence during which people coughed and cleared their throats but occasionally some idiot would start clapping all by himself and then several dozen heads would turn toward him as if to strike him with lightning. But now, in the car, there was no denying it: he was delighting in the music, moved to the very marrow of his bones as the trees and buildings along the avenue sparkled through the windshield, and this emotion was not only real but also the correct response.

In a burst of inspiration, he stopped at the stationery store where he usually bought his drafting materials and picked out some wrapping paper and ribbon. When he got home, Blanca wasn't there: a note on the dining-room table told him she'd gone to a job interview and would be back soon. If only he'd been paying attention, if only he'd noticed the chance repetition of certain names, coincidences that were already conspiring to wreak disaster upon him, while he, vigilant and inept, dazed, blind to what was irremediable, had seen nothing.

He was touched by Blanca's meticulous handwriting and the last word: "Kisses." For once he was glad she wasn't there. He cut the gleaming black wrapping paper down to size, wrapped up the two cassettes, folded the paper's corners with the skill and precision of an origami artist, calculated the exact length of gold ribbon required so the bow on the package wouldn't be tacky or ostentatious.

Absorbed in the task, he busied his hands within a circle of lamplight in the small room that was her domain and which they both called the studio, smoothing down the paper, sharpening its folds with a fingernail, sliding the tips of his index fingers and thumbs along the golden ribbon to make a knot that could be undone with a single tug.

He put the package away in a high cupboard with a certain exotic feeling of clandestinity, and that very night, at one minute past midnight, the first minute of Blanca's birthday, he couldn't stand the wait any longer and gave her the gift. This time he wasn't tortured by fear of having chosen the wrong thing, fear that Blanca wouldn't like it and would politely feign gratitude without fully concealing her disappointment. How clumsily she struggled to untie the package's golden knot, how nervously she tried to open the folds and edges of the paper! She ended up simply ripping it, and what a privilege to be standing in front of her and receive the full force of her eyes an instant after she saw the two cassettes. "Moncho, Twenty Classic

Boleros," she said, in the tone of voice she used only for unqualified rapture, for marveling gratitude, and that was one of the best reasons for loving her, because she intensely ennobled anything that she admired.

Blanca put one of the cassettes on immediately and turned to Mario as the first song began in an invitation to dance. But they didn't dance. They just stood in each other's arms in the middle of the room, slowly swaying without moving their feet, while Moncho sang *Llévatela—Take Her Away*. But no one would ever take her away, Mario thought in pride and desire, steering her gently toward the bedroom, letting her lead him there.

Five

THERE WOULD PROBABLY never be a re-
spite: he would have to spend every hour, every day
of the rest of his life winning her over, seducing
her, permanently on the lookout, astute and untir-
ing, for the appearance of any danger, any enemy.
That didn't bother him, of course; he'd known it
practically from the first moment he met her, and
when he stopped to think about it he had to admit
he hadn't done too badly since then. It had taken

him no more than two days to fall in love with Blanca, and the fact that she had begun, little by little, to have feelings for him, that she'd slowly slipped, without realizing it, from friendship and gratitude into love, was not the work of chance or the blind mechanism of passion, but the slow, hard-won result of Mario's tenacity, his constant, tender solicitude, as unconditional as a nurse's. In fact, that was what he'd been for a while, in the beginning: an assiduous nurse who cared for her with patience and skill, changed her sheets when they were soaked from long nights of delirium and fever, and little by little gave her back her strength and will to live. "You rebuilt me," Blanca once told him, "as if you'd found a porcelain vase that was smashed into a thousand pieces and you had the skill and patience to reconstruct the whole thing, down to the tiniest shard."

Mario, who appreciated almost nothing in life more than stability, had spent the past several years discovering and admiring Blanca's instabilities, while simultaneously trying to combat or attenuate them by offering her a place where her reference points were secure and her soul could flower, without waste or suffering, into its full splendor. With other men, or abandoned to her own devices, Blanca might drift—in fact, had already once drifted—into a dazed, painful, and sterile chaos, a kind of stupefied contemplation of her own disaster that contained an element of the fatalism with which a near-alcoholic, offered one last chance to go clean, gives in to the temptation to have another glass, or a somewhat untidy person suddenly abandons all attempt at daily hygiene and ends up living like an animal.

At the time Mario met her, Blanca drank six or seven vodkas per day, smoked two packs of Camels, and carried a purse stuffed with a confusion of dirty tissues, shreds of tobacco, loose rolling papers, and pills, both uppers and downers. Her life with the painter Naranjo, who'd initially dazzled her with his pretensions to genius and the visual force of his work, had quickly and foreseeably collapsed into a torturous hell of abandonments, reconciliations, disloyal acts, and abrupt departures that could have gone on for years had it not been for Mario's appearance.

People said, and Mario was sure it was true, that Blanca had played an important role in creating Naranjo's success. (Mario would have committed suicide before calling him "Jimmy.") Not only had she encouraged him, not only had she made him a better man, ennobling him with the beneficial influence of her admiration, she'd also used the very family influences she refused to resort to on her own behalf to find buyers for his paintings and convince galleries to show them. She'd marshaled her friends at newspapers and radio stations to interview him and write about his work, and had done so with a grace and tenacity that Naranjo himself lacked, or at least lacked then, when he was still pretending to be an antisocial *artiste maudit*, years before winning the Jaén Biennial and being converted to what he himself called, with the brazenly cynical mercantilism that passed for state-of-the-art modernity in the 1980s, *el bisnes*.

The energy Blanca would expend on behalf of other people's talents could be inexhaustible, even miraculous. And perhaps it was because she poured herself so generously into these external causes, Mario thought, that she lacked the drive to make herself into something, to carry through with any project of her own that would have required a concentrated effort of her will to complete. She had a very rare gift, the gift of admiration, and she knew how to explain what she admired and why she admired it with such conviction that her enthusiasm became contagious.

When she first met Naranjo in 1982 or '83, no one believed in his work, not even Naranjo. Blanca was the one who somehow convinced him that he truly was a painter and that the general indifference to his work wasn't due to the mediocrity of his paintings, as Naranjo himself had begun to think, but to the mediocrity of the audience, the incurable Spanish ignorance, the cultural wretchedness of the provinces. It was Blanca who dissuaded him from the grim temptation to take a government exam that could lead to a post as a professor of drawing. It was because of her that his work was entered into the competition for the Jaén City Council Biennial, in which Naranjo was refusing to participate, not only because it disgusted him to play along with power, as he was always saying, but also because he feared the humiliation of not being chosen. Without his knowledge—at that period he was generally lost in a haze of hashish and gin—Blanca chose one of his paintings and sent it to the Biennial, and she may also have spoken to one of the members of the jury about him, perhaps the very professor to whom she owed her lasting passion for Puccini. That last rumor was one she hotly denied, for even long after marrying Mario it infuriated her to hear anyone question Naranjo's talent. In any case it was clear that she did everything she could to promote her artist boyfriend's career, and in her own way she succeeded.

She was also the one who didn't let him be lulled into settling for local, provincial accolades. After the Jaén Biennial, he won the Zabaleta Prize, given by the municipal authorities of Quesada, and a few months later he was chosen to do the poster for the Baeza festival, which was a scandal in that very conservative city, a shocking rupture with the conventions that had governed that type of poster until then. In the province of Jaén, Naranjo became the radical personification of the avant-garde, but he would very likely have squandered this success if it hadn't been for Blanca's impassioned demands: he couldn't settle for what he'd already achieved, he had to make the definitive leap and become known in Granada, Madrid, across the wide world.

Without realizing it, she was working toward her own downfall. It was the contact with Madrid that finally sent Naranjo over the edge and transformed him into his abominable caricature Jimmy N., which sounded more like a disc jockey's name than a painter's. It wasn't always possible for Blanca to go with him on his trips to the nation's capital city, and though she was far too generous to be jealous on principle, as so many women are, she soon noticed that Naranjo was transforming at a dizzying rate, or perhaps showing his true colors.

News of his great triumph in Madrid spread all over Jaén, though it later became clear that word of said triumph had never actually reached Madrid. People were also talking about what they started to call his "Nuevo look." The crew-necked sweaters, work pants, and solid work boots of a proletarian realist or American abstract expressionist had been replaced by a wardrobe abundant in tight black leather garments and leopard- or zebra-print fabrics. He got rid of his beard and shaved his sideburns all the way up to the temples, for those were times in which the audacities of modernity seemed inseparable from a certain extravagance of hairstyle, and the selection of that hairstyle was as decisive in a person's life as the choice of a political ideology had been ten years earlier. Startled, then dumbfounded, and finally shattered by bitterness and a sense of betrayal, Blanca still couldn't bring herself to break up with him, and she attributed the most benign meaning she could to the new things she heard him say and saw him do, while trying not to pay too much attention to the pointy-toed shoes and newly acquired passion for disco music, parties, and cocaine. Even so, where he was concerned she was already starting to lose her habit of passionately adopting as her own the enthusiasms of a man she admired.

The Naranjo she'd fallen in love with was a gruff, taciturn artist, reserved to the point of claustrophobia and misanthropy, a steadfast communist, a user of hashish, but especially of alcohol, alien to all social conventions including employment, monogamy, paternity, scheduling, and the latest styles in painting, fond of finishing off his nights of bohemian revelry drinking pastis in the brothels, for in certain provincial intellectual circles of the time such inveterately masculine debauchery was celebrated as a statement of liberating marginality and dynamic dissidence. The Jimmy N. who began to emerge after the first trips to Madrid, the one who years later would shine forth in all his glory in the fashionable bars of Jaén, was an eccentric and rather effeminate diva, shamelessly addicted to the blandishments of power and money, dressed like a fashion model, but with the hard, ancient features of a man of the countryside, the faint shadow of a rural beard contrasting with the languid pallor that at the time was de rigueur. He began assembling an entourage of young disciples who constituted a vague art or design movement they called La Factory. They gave each other female nicknames and celebrated and repeated anything he said as if they were a kind of brainwashed sect, and indeed more than once they reminded Blanca of a band of Hare Krishnas. They were the ones who started calling him Jimmy N. and imitating his mannerisms and way of dressing, though it sometimes seemed as if he were imitating them which, given his age, was ridiculous in a way that was painfully visible even to Blanca's not always wide-open eyes. Now he declared himself a fan of cartoons and the most banal pop music hits, he who, only a little while before, would shut himself in his studio every morning to paint to the sound of blaring jazz, just like his hero, Jackson Pollock. During his black hours of discouragement, he'd often told Blanca that he'd rather burn his paintings or throw them on a garbage dump than humiliate himself by giving in to the demands of commercial art galleries, but now he liked to repeat a line that was very quickly copied and popularized by his disciples although, as Blanca discovered some time later, it hadn't even originated with him: "Time to wise up, Blanquita: the avant-garde is the marketplace."

On one of his first visits back from Madrid after setting up a studio there, Blanca overcame the cowardice of her love to ask him straight out whether he had another girlfriend. Naranjo, or rather Jimmy N., swore he didn't and seemed so hurt by her suspicions that he made her feel unfair, guilty, and contemptible. Without noticing how, she went from accuser to accused; instead of asking him for explanations she was begging his forgiveness. They managed to patch things up, and spent one more night of passion together that was almost like old times, except now they needed some help from cocaine, which was beginning to replace hashish on the cultural scale of prestige. It was a stimulant, not a relaxant; it promoted a speediness that was in keeping with the era; it was clean, smoke-free, residue-free, and instantaneous; it was said to arouse prodigious sexual desire; and furthermore, it did not create addiction, and had nothing to do with the laid-back hippy aura of hashish or the sordid manginess of heroin. . . .

They spent that weekend together and Naranjo left on Sunday night aboard the express train to Madrid. A few minutes before the train left, as they were saying good-bye, he winked at her and suggested in a low voice that they visit the train's restroom together. For a moment Blanca was flattered and surprised, thinking he might want to have a quick, wild fuck—a daring and almost impossible plan in that tiny space. But instead Naranjo asked her for the mirror she carried in her purse and made a couple of lines of cocaine on it with a recently acquired credit card. "If it were a Visa Gold card, the coke would taste even better," he said, passing his index finger along the edge of the card, then bringing it greedily to his mouth and extracting every last trace of pleasure out of the cocaine by rubbing it into his gums, his wide country-boy gums, as hard to conceal as the dark shadow of his beard or the Jaén accent that rose unchecked through the string of fashionable words, feminine diminutives, and pseudo-English terminology that threaded across his campy monologues.

When Blanca told him these stories, Mario felt as if they had happened in a different world from the one he knew, in some other city that couldn't be the same one where he lived. Before meeting her, he'd never heard of Jimmy Naranjo's fame or even his existence—which Blanca found very strange—and he'd never imagined that there were people in Jaén who used cocaine and lived such disorderly, bohemian lives.

Blanca had agreed to join Naranjo in Madrid a few days later to help him prepare for a long-awaited exhibit, his first solo show in the capital city. They'd agreed she would come up Friday night, but she couldn't wait that long. She caught the express twenty-four hours early, and at 7:30 Friday morning, one of those freezing Madrid winter mornings, she emerged from a taxi and opened the door of the studio, a former pharmaceutical warehouse on Calle Augusto Figueroa that Naranjo had immediately started calling *el loft*, and that he could never have rented to begin with had it not been for a providential check from Blanca's mother.

By the dawn glow that came in through a vast skylight, Blanca saw Naranjo naked and on his knees next to the bed, around which unframed canvases and paint-stained drop cloths hung like curtains in a theater. When he heard the key in the lock, Naranjo had raised his head from between the open knees of someone who was lying back on the bed, a very young boy whose face Blanca didn't glimpse because she turned and ran outside without even slamming the door, afraid that if she looked back her eyes would see again something she'd never wanted to see, something she'd never forget.

Six

SHORTLY AFTER THAT she met Mario. In an inscription written in a book she gave him for their first anniversary, Blanca alluded to the sad state she'd been in and her gratitude to Mario by citing these lines from Rafael Alberti:

Cuando tú apareciste
Penaba yo en la entraña más profunda
De una cueva sin aire y sin salida.

When you appeared
I was agonizing in the deepest cavern
Of a cave with no air and no exit.

They met, she sometimes said, against all
odds, on one of the rare occasions when their separate worlds happened to coincide, for even in
small cities and state capitals as provincial as Jaén
the people who brush past each other in the street
live at interplanetary distances from one another:
even when their paths cross it's very difficult for
them to actually see each other.

In order for it to happen, Mario had to turn
up one night in the kind of place he never went,
a newly opened club called Chinatown, housed
in a former convent, with laser beams, stacks of
video screens, and monolithic black speakers blast-
ing pounding rhythms. One of the department
heads had to have a bachelor party, in order for
Mario—so befuddled by the music, the lights, and
the crowd that he couldn't locate his co-workers,
for they were the ones who'd gotten him into this

pickle, as always, practically dragging him to this hellish spot after a dinner that had already been unbearable in and of itself—to be standing at the fluorescent bar of that discothèque holding a lukewarm gin and tonic and trying to hear or say something to a girl he'd been introduced to a while before, whose name (because of the noise and the gin) he wasn't sure he remembered.

Blanca told him later, when they compared notes in an attempt to reorganize the initial muddled episodes of their shared past, that she couldn't remember his name either. In her case it wasn't only the loud music, but also the abuse of alcohol, cocaine, and pills that, combined with perpetual sleep deprivation, had weakened her memory, especially her verbal memory, to the point that she'd be talking and suddenly find herself unable to think of a word, or be on the point of saying someone's name to find that she'd forgotten it. Words were missing, hours of her life were missing, sometimes a step was missing when she was going down a staircase and suddenly she'd be overcome with vertigo and know that she couldn't go on living like that.

Mario didn't know it at the time, but the monitors were playing a video clip about Jimmy N.'s latest show, which had opened in triumph a few days earlier in the galleries of the Savings and Loan, from where, the rumor went, it would be traveling a few weeks later to New York (and indeed, with an eye to the indispensable American market, the clip was narrated in English). The bank's Office of Cultural Programs had spared no expense in producing the video, which was cofinanced by the Cultural Council of Andalucía. The music hadn't actually been composed by Santiago Auserón, as was claimed in the opening credits, but was indeed by a very close collaborator of his, and the footage had been commissioned from a director of TV advertisements who'd won prizes at several international festivals.

By then Blanca had broken up with Naranjo two or three times, but that night she couldn't muster the willpower to keep from going to Chinatown in the hope of seeing him. She was almost trembling when she got there, already regretting that she'd come, and then all her fear of running into him, which she hadn't lost even after drinking a vodka straight up, turned to disappointment when she learned that Naranjo had just left. The presentation of the video had been a huge success, one of his disciples who'd stayed behind to keep on eye on subsequent showings told her with effeminate rapture. Everyone had been there, the *most high*, he said in English, the Municipal Cultural Councillor, the Provincial Representative of the regional government, the Vice President of the Savings and Loan, it was overflowing with VIPs in here, chortled the pale, shaven-headed Hare Krishna acolyte in his heavy black clothes and heavy black shoes with thick rubber soles, his temples so closely shaven that they were blue.

Blanca tried hard to keep from nursing a growing resentment, a petty bitterness about being left out of the picture just when Naranjo was beginning to enjoy a success that wouldn't have been possible without her. But she knew that success tends to separate artists from the people who supported them during their early obscurity. She still felt a reluctant but obsessive love for Naranjo, in which her memories of pleasure and of their former intellectual alliance played no role whatsoever: it was nothing but the pure inertia of love, its indestructible tendency to outlast everything else, beyond comfort, beyond reason, even beyond Blanca's own desires, for after the scene in the Madrid studio she was sure she could never go to bed with Naranjo again. Steeling up her courage, fully prepared to understand and accept, she'd asked him if he'd fallen in love with that boy. She wasn't at all ready for his reaction. Naranjo burst out laughing, looked at her as if she were an idiot he was continually having to reproach for the naive vulgarity of her middle-class upbringing, and said, "What do you mean 'in love'? He was a rent boy from Calle Almirante."

She knew she was never going to be able to trust him again, but if Naranjo had come to her and made promises or tearfully proffered some improbable declaration—"It wasn't what you were imagining," as if it were something she'd merely imagined and not seen with her own eyes—Blanca would have gone against the dictates of her dignity and intelligence in order to believe or try to believe him, successfully sustaining the illusion until the next betrayal. She took tranquilizers to fall asleep and stimulants to wake up; she made it through the days on endless cigarettes, vodkas, and coffees, in a stupefied haze of lassitude, bodily malaise, and desolation. She would wake up at 5:00 a.m. to find the television still on, and sometimes when she bumped into doorframes or hallway corners she'd realize that her walk was as lurching and unsteady as a drunk's.

Standing at the bar in Chinatown that night, she'd barely noticed Mario's face and would never have had any further recollection of his existence if not for the fact that after a disjointed and practically shouted conversation—during which she never stopped looking around in case Naranjo reappeared—she started feeling sick. Thinking this was caused by the dense heat in the crowded room, she asked Mario to please excuse her, she was going outside to get a little fresh air and would be right back. A few minutes later, tired of waiting and exhausted by the noise and people, Mario went outside himself, on his way home. He found her on the sidewalk, doubled over between two cars with one hand pressed against her stomach while the other held onto her hair, vomiting and moaning, her body convulsed at regular intervals by violent shudders.

He pushed her hair back and wiped the glistening sweat from her face. Lots of people were standing around the bar's doorway but no one seemed to have noticed them. He led her over to some front steps a short distance away and helped her sit down. For a moment she thought it was Naranjo who was helping her and threw her arms around his neck and held him, trembling, as she repeated a name that was completely unknown to Mario. He gently maneuvered her away from him, not only because he felt awkward about receiving caresses intended for someone else but also because Blanca's breath was an acid stench of alcohol, nicotine, and vomit.

A few minutes later she leaned back with her eyes closed, somewhat calmer but still clutching Mario's hand. Her own hands, whose softness was delicious to him, were unusually cold. Suddenly her nails dug into his palm and she went rigid: she'd just started to look for something, her pack of cigarettes, undoubtedly, and realized that she'd lost her purse. She became frantic, as in those situations of panic and powerlessness that happen in dreams, wildly enumerating the things she thought she'd lost, though without doing anything more to try and find them than grope blindly around her: her house keys, her ID card, her ATM card, the silver lighter that someone, another male name, had given her....

It didn't take Mario long to find the purse. It had been dropped next to the sidewalk, back where he'd first spotted her between the two cars, and it was still there, splattered with vomit. The drinkers milling around the entrance to the bar had passed by without noticing it, stepping in vomit as indifferently, thought Mario, as they'd have stepped on her if she hadn't been able to get up. He'd always felt a vague but aggressive hostility toward the denizens of nightclubs, and not just toward their way of dressing, speaking, and holding glasses and cigarettes. It was the hatred of the earlybird for the night owl, deeply rooted in him from the beginning, perhaps inherited from his father, who had risen before dawn his whole life to go out and work in the fields, and who was now languishing in an old people's home in Linares.

Another thing he'd inherited from his father was his immaculate neatness: he wiped the purse clean with a tissue before handing it back to Blanca. Her hands were shaking so badly as she opened it that everything spilled out and she couldn't find what she was looking for: her cigarettes and the lighter. She repeated that it was a silver Zippo and was once again overcome with remorse at having lost it. Kneeling on the sidewalk, she searched around with long, clumsy, nervous fingers, oblivious to the feet of the people who were going by, blindly rummaging, without seeing even Mario. She looked for it just as she would always look for everything, the most valuable objects and the most trivial, even after she had been living with Mario for a long time: very nervous and irritated—as if, in the anarchy of the insides of drawers, the objects had conspired among themselves to mock her— and fearing that she'd lost forever just the thing she needed most, the book she had to read, the first pages of something she was at last beginning to write that, once she'd lost them, left her back at the same point of departure as always, a dispirited tangle of projects, none of them entirely anchored in reality. She finally found a cigarette, a single, bent cigarette, and put it between her lips while still searching for the lighter, but it was Mario who spotted it and offered her a light.

"If you smoke you'll feel even worse," he said.

"I couldn't possibly feel worse."

"Come on, calm down. I'll get you a glass of water."

"Don't go." Blanca gripped him. "Don't leave me alone."

Both of them would have been surprised to learn that before much more time had passed he would be promising never to leave her alone again. That night he took her back to her house in a taxi—she couldn't remember the address but he found an envelope in her purse that was printed with it—and at the entrance to the building Blanca asked him to come up, clinging to him with the same anguish as a while earlier when she was afraid he was going to go for a glass of water. The apartment, part of which was also the former studio of Jimmy N., looked catastrophic to Mario: a perverse mixture of filth and disorder, sordid domesticity and vaguely bohemian set design, like a movie showing how artists used to suffer in the olden days. Blanca walked across the whole apartment turning on all the lights as if she were afraid someone were there or as if she were still hoping Naranjo had come back. In the bedroom where, as in all the rooms, canvases leaned against the wall and newspapers and posters were strewn everywhere, the very large bed was unmade and the sheets were visibly dirty, thought Mario. On the night table was an overflowing ashtray, a glass half-full of water and a small bottle of capsules whose label Mario examined with some concern. On the wall over the bed, a large unframed canvas, carelessly held in place with thumb tacks and staples, bore a muddled shape that it took Mario some time to recognize as a body, and then as a naked female body, and a face that, despite the brush strokes that disfigured it as if it were reflected in murky and turbulent waters, was Blanca's face. For some reason it intimidated him to find himself simultaneously in the presence of a woman and a painting that showed her naked, even though her nakedness was rendered almost unrecognizable by the painting's style, which Mario dared to conjecture was expressionist—or perhaps by the painter's inability to correctly reproduce an image.

Blanca sat down on the bed, rummaged through the drawer of the night table, slammed it shut, then poked through the ashtray until she located a cigarette that was almost intact—she must have put it out only seconds after lighting it the night before. The reek of old cigarette smoke and sheets long unchanged was sickening. Mario, who didn't like visiting other people's houses, had an unpleasant feeling that he was invading someone's intimate privacy. What right did he have to be there, with a woman who was a complete stranger, at two in the morning, in a bedroom in which there were ostensible signs of the presence of another male? What was he doing there when the woman, Blanca, whom he was already beginning to like, seemed to have forgotten his presence entirely? Not daring to step inside, he stood in the doorway of the bedroom and watched her bury her head between her knees, perched on the edge of the bed with a trail of smoke still ascending on one side. He noticed that she was shaking and was afraid she was about to vomit again. But this time she was shaking because she was crying, silently, in hard, dry sobs that were as alien to Mario as was the cigarette she was holding between her fingers. Afraid she'd set the sheets on fire, Mario approached her, timid and cautious, took the cigarette away, and put it out with disgust in the ashtray. Blanca lifted her eyes and seemed not to remember who he was. At moments, Mario's compassion was already turning to tenderness. By now he found her much, much prettier than he had a few hours earlier when they were introduced.

"What do you think, shall I make some coffee?" he said, trying to make his voice sound natural and relaxed, the voice of a man who's used to going out at night and spending lots of time with women and artists. Blanca managed to focus her eyes on him and moved her head in a gesture that looked like nodding.

There wasn't a plate, spoon, or cup that wasn't dirty in that kitchen, and that hadn't been dirty for at least a week. The sink was hard to find beneath the pile of filthy dishes. When he managed to rescue the coffeepot and began trying to wash it out, Mario discovered that the water had been cut off. And of course there were no bottles of water in the refrigerator stored up in case of the usual restrictions. All that was there were a container of rancid margarine and an unopened bottle of mayonnaise, along with a moldy tomato. Mario, like all very orderly people, was not only appalled by this disaster but felt reaffirmed and almost smug in his own habits. He went back to the bedroom to tell Blanca he couldn't make coffee and found her asleep, on her side, facing the light on the night table, her two hands holding the pillow, her legs pulled up against her stomach, breathing through her mouth, with sweat gleaming on her upper lip. She hadn't even taken off her shoes. Very carefully, Mario removed them and then slowly pulled the blanket up to her chin, trying not to wake her, watching her sleep with a delight all the more intense for being furtive. He thought about leaving her a note on the nightstand or even on the bathroom mirror as he'd seen in the movies, but he wasn't carrying paper or pen, and in any case had no idea what to write. He was tempted to leave her one of his cards but decided against it just in time; that would have been, he later considered, far too commercial and impertinent a gesture. He stood there for a minute or two more, watching Blanca sleep, without knowing what to do, what strategy to come up with so the night's accidental connection wouldn't be lost. But he lacked experience as well as shrewdness and was suddenly afraid that the man she'd called out to once or twice in her delirium, the owner of the three or four masculine articles strewn about the house, would unexpectedly appear and place him in an ambiguous and even dangerous situation....

His heart jumped at the sound of an elevator. When he went closer to Blanca so as to switch off the lamp on the nightstand, he felt like kissing her on the lips. She opened her eyes, still asleep, shivered, repeated the other man's name. Mario turned off the bedroom light and then went around the apartment switching off all the other lights with his incorrigible instinct for thrift. It was three in the morning when he got back out to the street. He walked home, a little dazed by the strangeness of being awake and out in the street at that hour, and with a feeling of novelty and gratification, as if he were living out the first draft of an as yet indeterminate adventure. Then he realized he hadn't even taken the precaution of jotting down Blanca's phone number.

Seven

HE SPENT THE weekend wondering what to do next and trying to figure out the best way to get in touch with Blanca again. At the age of 28, Mario's sentimental education was extremely limited. Until he was 25, he'd had a girlfriend he planned to marry. She left him a few months before the wedding, undoubtedly out of sheer boredom though she claimed she'd fallen in love with someone else. Everyone likes to attribute noble motives to their actions, and Juli, Mario's girlfriend, who'd been going out with him for seven years at that point, must have thought an illicit love affair was a more solid and prestigious justification for breakup than mere tedium. They'd shared one of those eternal provincial relationships that begin at the end of adolescence and end a decade later in a marriage that is lethargic from before the start, so inevitable and immutable that it's closer to the realm of nature than to the feelings and actions of human beings, one of those relationships whose future is even more unvarying than its past: not only the white dress at the door of the church, the apartment with the brand-new imitation-oak furniture, the honeymoon in Mallorca or the Canary Islands immediately followed by a pregnancy, but also the deeply buried mutual suspicion of having been swindled, the bored bitterness of Sunday strolls with or without a baby carriage, the sweet, familial stupor, so much like the dull, heavy feeling that follows a big meal.

For Juli to have had the uncommon fortitude to break up with Mario and invent a nonexistent infidelity as justification were both strong indicators of the degree of boredom and disillusionment they'd sunk into over the years. Mario took the humiliation of being dumped rather badly at first and tended to confuse his displeasure with the sufferings of love. He wrote several supplicating or insulting letters, amply stocked with literary clichés; he pondered the inconstancy of women and spent a few afternoons wandering around the building where his ex-girlfriend worked, with the rather melodramatic notion of surprising her with his rival—a word much in vogue then on the popular Latin American soap operas. He also feared the vague rural opprobrium attached to bachelors—"old boys," as his mother used to say.

Then, after summer vacation, he began realizing he could spend whole days without thinking of her once, and shortly thereafter he privately acknowledged that he'd never really missed her. The apartment he'd bought to share with her now struck him as a very pleasant place to live alone. Raised in a large, unmodernized house in a country village, a house that smelled like a stable and was glacially cold in winter, Mario was gratefully appreciative of hot water, clean bathrooms, the luxury of central heating. He chose furniture to please himself alone, though the suspicious looks he got from the salespeople made him uncomfortable; it must have been unusual for a single man to be furnishing a house with such care. He practiced a painless austerity in order to keep up with his monthly mortgage payments without anxiety; he got a membership at a video rental place, and joined a book-of-the-month club. It was then that he remembered his schoolboy affinity for history and bought Menéndez Pidal's *History of Spain* on the installment plan. He embarked on a plan to read it from the first volume to the last, and would always remember that he had made it to the obscure and tedious reign of the Visigoths when he met Blanca. At the Council they thanked him for his first three years on the job. He started working some afternoons in the architectural studio a few former boardingschool classmates of his had started, and he'd sometimes venture forth at night with one of them to drink wine in one or another of the city's bars, with some vague idea of getting drunk and picking up girls. But they never managed to do either of those things, and after a while, bored and disappointed with each other, they stopped going out together. Shortly thereafter Mario's old friend "got to be boyfriends" as they say in Jaén, with the studio's secretary, a rather heavyset young woman who was so unappealing that Mario secretly felt some pity for his former friend. Better to be alone than to resign yourself so halfheartedly to a woman like that.

He watched his expenses so carefully that of the two paychecks he received per month, he could put the entire second one away in savings. His parents, now retired, lived alone back in the village, and his only brother, eight years older, was a first sergeant in the Guardia Civil stationed in Irún. Mario felt a strong obligation to bring his parents to live with him in Jaén, but though he had a great deal of affection for them, especially for his mother, he was also aware that they were fast approaching the infirmities of old age and within a few short years their company would become a kind of slavery. One day, in an unprecedented gesture, his father called him at the office and solemnly announced that he and his mother were going to be moving into a Social Security residence in Linares the following month.

The news made Mario so happy that he felt like a loathsome ingrate. He said sincerely, on the point of tears and with a tightness in his chest, that as long as he could take care of them that was not going to happen. When she got on the line, his mother was crying: it's best for everyone this way, she repeated, in the same words as his father; this way neither of them would ever become a burden. That weekend, Mario drove back to his village and took his parents to the residence, which was a spacious establishment, clean and melancholy, with a modern chapel, bedrooms that seemed to belong in a youth hostel, and a surprising degree of liveliness in the cafeteria and common rooms.

Night fell as he was driving back to Jaén on Sunday, sadly listening to the radio, the results of the day's sports events, ads for cognac and cigars. But it was the weightless and fundamentally healthful sadness of freedom that he was feeling. When he stepped into his apartment that night, it seemed to belong to him entirely for the first time, as did his future, in which he would no longer be tied down by attachments to his early youth, his parents, his girlfriend, and his oppressive memories of Cabra de Santocristo, to which he would certainly never return since there was no longer anyone there for him to visit. With serene approval of his own practical decisions, he looked over the still scant furnishings, the spotless kitchen, the row of volumes of Menéndez Pidal's *History of Spain*, the bedroom once intended for a couple but where now he slept alone, the few light fixtures he had installed. He had dinner at the kitchen table without falling into the lax habits of those who eat any old way when they're alone. He cleared off the table after dinner and washed and dried the plates, glass, and silverware. He started watching a movie on TV and fell asleep on the sofa before it was over. At midnight the phone woke him up. Only when he discovered it was a wrong number did he realize how much he'd wanted to talk to someone that Sunday night. He switched off the TV and straightened up the dining room a little, though almost nothing was out of place, brushed his teeth, rinsed the brush and carefully recapped the toothpaste, chose a clean pair of pajamas out of the closet that was far too big for him alone, and slipped with anticipated pleasure between the sheets, which he'd changed on Friday afternoon before going back to his village. He switched off the light still thinking he was overcome with drowsiness, but as he lay in the dark he realized that for some reason he was no longer sleepy at all. He turned the light back on: he'd forgotten to plug in the alarm clock, an unnecessary precaution he was always careful to take, though he woke up automatically every morning around 7:15.

A few weeks later, standing in line at the bank, he ran into Juli. Neither of them knew what to say at first; she turned red and nervous, and Mario was stunned to realize that he had lost all interest in her in so little time. He thought she looked older than she was, a bit old-fashioned and tacky in her checked skirt and high burgundy boots, carrying a black plastic file with the logo of the Nuestra Señora de la Cabeza Driving School and Agency in gold letters. They talked for a few minutes while Mario waited for his turn at the window. Juli—suddenly her name struck him as ridiculous—told him she'd thought about him a lot and didn't want to lose touch: they could call each other sometimes and chat like old friends. Mario made a display of going along with this, but was quick-witted enough to put off the meeting she was proposing to some indefinite future moment. It was a relief to leave the bank and not see her. If Juli hadn't broken up with him, they would have gotten married a month earlier. How strange, he thought, as he want back to the office; I was on the verge of marrying a total stranger. I suffered over a woman I didn't actually like much;

I spent seven years with her without getting to know a thing about her.

They didn't see each other again. She may have moved to another city or gone back to the village; she always used to say that big noisy places like Jaén wore her out. Mario believed for years that Juli had vanished from his memory without a trace and had played no role at all in the destiny that took him to Blanca. Only much later, in the choking fullness of his misery, did he think again of his first girlfriend and the future with her that had not come about, and he was afraid that out of some colossal misunderstanding, some fundamental error in the laws governing the world, someone had assigned him a biography that wasn't really his, a marriage to a woman who was obviously far better suited to another man, perhaps neither the painter Naranjo nor the scoundrel Onésimo, but in any case another man who was not Mario, a man who was taller, blonder, better educated, better traveled, more imaginative, more like her, not a draftsman at the Jaén Provincial Council whose expectations of life were compatible not with Blanca's—however hard both of them tried to make them compatible and believe that they were—but with those of the secretary of a driving school, the type of woman Juli precisely personified: a woman who would never suffer because she couldn't attend the Bienniale di Venezia or the premiere of *Madame Butterfly* in Covent Garden in London, a woman who wouldn't have known a thing about modern art or opera or Covent Garden, but without therefore being an idiot or a mental bureaucrat, as Blanca so often said, as if there were dishonor in being a bureaucrat....

On his worst days, during his blackest diatribes against himself, through the many sleepless nights when he lay in the dark next to the inviolate distance that separated him from Blanca, Mario would torment himself with the thought that he should have married Juli, should have arranged a time to get together with her as she'd suggested when they ran into each other in the bank. He accused himself of senseless arrogance, masculine vanity and ambition, of aspiring to things that were out of his reach; he imagined himself coldly leaving Blanca and going off in search of Juli, calculating that if he hadn't broken up with her they'd have a child or two by now, and in his embittered delirium he imagined the life he would have had with another woman so vividly that he couldn't help starting to feel as if he were betraying Blanca. Then he was frightened by the danger of never having met Blanca at all, and to make up for these thoughts and console himself he'd plunge deep into the unlimited memory of all the things he'd enjoyed thanks to her and with her, comparing those years of enthusiasm and passion with the years of conjugal stability and paternity he would have been living out with Juli as routinely as he served out the years of his employment at the Council.

It wasn't only that he was crazy about Blanca, that he liked her better than any other woman he saw in any part of reality, including movies and advertisements, and that his desire could be aroused by nothing more than the memory of her naked body or by brushing against her in the kitchen as they were washing the dishes. It was that in all the years of his life he had only ever been in love with her, so that his idea of love was inseparable from Blanca's existence, and since he had now known love and no longer knew how to do without it and didn't imagine that other women could offer it to him, there was nothing for him to do but go on living with her, under whatever conditions—he understood this almost at the end, vanquished, perhaps unworthy, more in love than ever—whatever conditions Blanca, or the stranger or shadow who had supplanted her, wanted to dictate.

What he most bitterly reproached himself for was his lack of vigilance and cunning, his excessive confidence not in the love or fidelity of Blanca, whom he would never reproach for anything, but in male nature, or the abject version of it represented by the individual whose name Mario had heard and read several times without paying attention to it, without realizing that the only real danger emanated from him. Did he first see the name Lluís

Onésimo in one of the cultural supplements that Blanca went through so avidly on Saturday mornings over breakfast, did he hear it on television, in that program *Metrópolis* that he always fell asleep halfway through, or was it Blanca's own sacred lips that had formed its syllables for the first time, with the same reverent and entirely unmerited generosity with which she pronounced so many names that awoke no echo but ignorance and hostility in Mario, names of artists, directors, choreographers, or vile, conceited writers whom she approached after their readings, asking them in her warm and admiring voice to sign a copy of their book for her or talk for a few minutes, men just in from Madrid with the smell of tobacco and whisky on their breath and eyes that would invariably move toward Blanca's neckline or give her a sidelong glance as she held out the book for them to sign as if she were offering up her whole life on a platter.

Animosity sharpened his memory: the first time he heard the name Lluís Onésimo was an ordinary Tuesday in June, a day like all the other sweet monotonous days of his vanished happiness, and he even remembered the first course of the meal Blanca had made, a *vichyssoise*, and that the TV news was going on about Frida Kahlo, which alarmed him because he didn't yet know that Blanca, in one of her impetuous aesthetic shifts, had ceased, from one day to the next, to be interested in Frida Kahlo, and that very soon, fatally drawn by the gravitational pull of Onésimo's intellectualism, she would abjure what the villainous multimedia artist from Valencia disdainfully called the "traditional supports." The era of classic formats, canvas, oil, even acrylic, had come to an end, the era of the Painter with a capital P, elitist and exclusive, was over, and had never been more than a holdover from the nineteenth century, a parody whose pathetic extreme was now embodied by the obsolete Jimmy N.

Those were the things Mario heard Lluís Onésimo say during the first meal they shared on the day Blanca introduced them to each other, and though he understood none of it and disliked the artist's looks and even his exaggerated accent, Mario took base satisfaction in the belittlement of his former rival Naranjo, and observed with tenderness, pity, and almost remorse that when she heard those words Blanca lowered her head and pressed her lips together, and didn't dare defend the man she had so recently admired.

With painful lucidity, with the retrospective bitterness of not having guessed in time, Mario realized far too late that Blanca's sudden lack of interest in Frida Kahlo, which had come as such a relief, was a clue to the fact that she had just developed a gigantic new admiration: she'd learned everything about Onésimo in the art magazines and the *El País* Sunday supplement, she'd read the articles about what she called his installations and performances, and with all the fervor of a recent convert she'd admired his public statements, which were often scandalous, his shaved head, his perennial three-day stubble, his black clothing, the vaguely Asiatic tattoo on the back of his right hand, his rings. She had thought, with an intolerable sense of having been treated unfairly and passed over, that she would never have the chance to see one of Lluís Onésimo's installations in person or attend one of his performances, and she had imagined the impossible gift of the wonder of a conversation with him, a very long conversation, lasting all night, with cigarettes and drinks, about art, and movies no one in Jaén had seen, and books no one in the whole city but her had read. And suddenly one day, one of those smoothly monotonous days that Mario so cherished, Blanca read in the local paper that Lluís Onésimo was preparing an exhibit and lecture for the Cultural Center of the Savings and Loan, and so she could go talk to him, could even offer to help him install his work, willing and enthusiastic, rapturous, uncontainable. The minute he saw them standing together, after enduring Onésimo's nonstop verbiage and nauseating table manners for two hours—strange that Blanca who was generally such a stickler hadn't seemed to notice—Mario López thought with clairvoyant dread that this ill-favored individual was going to seduce Blanca away from him.

Eight

WHAT VANITY COULD have made him take Blanca's love for granted? What mindless blindness could have led him to believe he was out of danger and their life together would go serenely on forever, the way a job does once the civil service entrance exam has been passed? Perhaps Blanca's indirect accusation was right: he, Mario, had become a mental bureaucrat; he'd thought getting married was like getting a permanent government position, like his job as draftsman at the Council, where he gradually accumulated experience, routine, and three-year review periods. Blanca never stopped by the office to see him or showed any interest in meeting any of his fellow workers. Mario had learned to resist the temptation to tell her about the little things that happened at work, disagreements with superiors or the petty intrigues of co-workers looking to advance another rung up the ladder. He'd start in with a story and notice that Blanca was distracted or, even worse, was smiling and nodding without paying much attention, and then he was afraid of boring her or seeming banal and he'd try to think of another topic of conversation or ask her what she'd done all morning and whom she'd seen.

But Blanca never gave a very precise account of her daily life. In almost everything she did say about herself and her feelings and desires, and in everything she told him about her past, there was a vagueness, an area of mystery she never clarified and that Mario didn't always dare question her about.

It had been that way from the start, from their very first encounters, and Mario was not unaware that the aura of uncertainty that surrounded Blanca's life and actions was as powerful an allure as physical desire in the rapid crystallization of his love. The more he wanted her the more he also wanted to know about her, but neither form of desire was ever fully satisfied, which made them all the more urgent to Mario who, for the first time in his life, at a late age and without prior experience, was discovering the upheavals and hypnotic effects of love.

He'd go looking for Blanca and not find her, wander around her building for a while and then give up, trail disconsolately back home, and find her there waiting for him in the entryway. He didn't know what it was that drove him to look for her, and he didn't understand what other reasons she had for trying to avoid him. She fell sick from depression and anemia, from the fearsome disarray of her daily life, and Mario, still no more than an obliging friend, keeping his love a secret, took care of her, used his administrative skills to help her sort through the disaster of her Social Security paperwork, managed to get the electric company to reconnect her after her power was cut off for nonpayment—without prior notification, she claimed. Under a mountain of assorted papers, old newspapers, and more than one pair of dirty underwear, Mario found the electric company's warning notices, all unopened.

Little by little, almost furtively, he was making himself indispensable. When she was at her lowest point, so depressed and weakened she could barely get out of bed, Mario took three personal days off and spent them taking care of her and cleaning up her house, which was a more exhausting task than he could have foreseen but which left him, when he'd finished, with a very pleasant feeling of personal satisfaction, though he wasn't sure whether Blanca had noticed any of the effort he had gone to. He bought detergents, sponges, window cleaners, polishes, disinfectants, mops, replacement mop heads, scouring pads, dish towels. He went to the home and kitchen section of the local Pryca and came back with the car fully loaded. He understood that Blanca had grown up in a household staffed with servants, raised in the belief that other people would take care of the housework, and he imagined, as well, with some degree of jealous spite, that Naranjo had been an incorrigible slob, taking the same approach to his own personal hygiene as to his canvases.

Blanca probably hadn't had a proper meal for months before they met, "*una comida como Dios manda,*" as Mario would say, repeating one of his mother's favorite expressions: a meal as God ordains. He talked to his mother over the phone two or three times a week, hearing her voice gradually turn into an old lady's voice that seemed to come from very far away and that overwhelmed him with guilt and tenderness. It was his mother's specialties that Mario knew best how to make, and he began preparing them for Blanca; cooking for her gave him a satisfying sense of himself as a skilled and diligent man that turned into something close to euphoria when she, at first so listless and uninterested, willingly ate up a plateful of lentil stew or chicken with rice and told him she'd never tasted anything so good.

He got used to living for Blanca, adapting his schedule to her needs, her sudden whims and outbursts. He enjoyed a kind of furtive and half-clandestine happiness, a happiness sustained by Blanca's mere presence but continually assailed by crises of dejection and fear. The phone would ring and he'd be afraid the call was from Naranjo; someone would knock at the door and he'd go to answer, drying his hands on his apron and thinking he might see the painter's hated face in front of him for the first time, afraid Naranjo's arrival would expel him from the delicate, ambiguous situation he'd grown so accustomed to. He was more than a friend but not a lover, simply a kind of helpful figure, and he was afraid Blanca's only feeling toward him was gratitude. Sometimes she'd look at him and seem to see not him but someone else.

He was ashamed of desiring her so much, ashamed of spying on her with primal hunger. She had moments of carelessness that plunged him into secret torments of an asphyxiating lust as strong as what he'd felt during his shadowy rural adolescence. Blanca would step out of the shower without having closed the bathroom door and he'd see her naked and white in the steam, tall and slim yet shapely, as elegant and exciting, he thought, as the models pictured in magazines, and so different from Juli, whose small, compact body he remembered only very dimly. Every morning he took a glass of fresh orange juice to her in bed, and when she sat up, still half-dozing, her face deliciously puffy after her first nights of deep, unbroken sleep in a very long time, the sheet would slip off her shoulders and reveal her small round breasts, which he barely glimpsed before averting his eyes in embarrassment, and Blanca would cover herself up unconcernedly as she drank the juice, then fall back to sleep.

The stronger his desire, the more excessive his love, the stiffer he grew. He became more and more timid with her, ever clumsier and more obliging, trying to make up with efficiency and practical assistance for what he felt to be his lack of attractiveness, the mediocre stature of everything he felt himself to be and to have in comparison to what Blanca deserved, what Blanca expected. Sometimes he thought she was aware of his anguished desire and was not flattered by it, only compassionate and detached. One night when he was about to leave, after they'd stayed up talking and drinking gin and tonic until very late—nowadays she allowed herself only a single gin and tonic every once in a while, and had Mario pour the gin—Blanca asked him to stay a little longer, and he was shaken with thrilled panic, imagining that now, at last, something that never happened was finally going to happen. After an instant's hesitation, he sat down next to her on the sofa, not across from her as he'd been until then, and even that modest audacity almost made him dizzy.

"I'll never be able to thank you for all you're doing for me," said Blanca with a serious smile and a confiding, intimate look that he thought perhaps he should bemoan, for he suspected that this was the lukewarm intimacy of someone who was not in love. "I'll never be able to make it up to you."

"But you've already made it up to me." Mario was unexpectedly carried away by a torrent of eloquence. "No one has ever given me as much as you have; you've made me discover life. I feel as if I've been sleeping until now and you've finally woken me up. What was I doing when I met you? Working and meeting my monthly payments and reading the *History of Spain* every night. I was asleep and didn't know it, and if it weren't for you I could have grown old and never woken up at all, ever."

"When I'm falling asleep at night," she said, "I often hope I'll never wake up."

"I thought you were feeling better lately." Mario was suddenly crushed by the thought that all his effort to care for Blanca had been in vain, that he hadn't even managed to alleviate the sense of disaster and despair that had shocked him about her the night they met. Maybe she still missed Naranjo; she might even be trying to call him when Mario wasn't there, when he went back to his own apartment at night after washing the dishes like some eunuch butler.

Sitting so close to her on the sofa, exalted by the two gin and tonics he'd drunk, he thought that instead of paying so much attention to what she was saying he ought to take her in his arms and kiss her, really kiss her, on the mouth, not just the two polite little pecks dictated by protocol that he always gave her. But he didn't do it, and went home as he always did, more depressed and disgusted with himself each time.

Back home, he couldn't sleep. He didn't sleep at all that whole night, didn't have a second's relief in the darkness or when he switched on the light. He masturbated anxiously and without pleasure, trying to concentrate on Blanca's half-glimpsed nakedness, and ended up feeling the same shame as when he was a teenager. He was frightened by the reality of a pain he'd never experienced before, and that he couldn't find a way to ward it off. Why was he so determined to go on seeing Blanca? Why did he imagine that being with her was the only possible way to achieve not even happiness, but simple calm, when in fact what he felt in her presence was a permanent state of insecurity, anguish, and regret for not daring to say and do what he wanted, or for having said or done something that might strike her as ridiculous or trivial?

He'd be better off not seeing her again. At eight the next morning, with a deceptive feeling of lightness and lucidity caused by lack of sleep, Mario arrived at the office before anyone else and sat down in front of his drawing table, prepared to return to his senses and focus all the considerable force of his will on forgetting Blanca, getting her out of his system, he said, using an expression that until very recently had not been part of his vocabulary, and that reminded him unpleasantly of cocaine and that charlatan nincompoop Naranjo (against whom he stockpiled adjectives as if they were projectiles Mario could hurl at him or spells that would keep him from reentering Blanca's life).

He managed to go four whole days without calling her. Years later, in his blackest hours of jealousy and defeat, he would reflect with astonishment and a trace of cynicism upon the fact that it hadn't been all that hard to pull away from her. Perhaps at that point he didn't yet love her as much as he thought he did. In fact, he wasn't the one who brought about their next meeting. One morning at precisely ten o'clock as he was on his way back from his coffee break, one of his colleagues passed him in the corridor and said with a wink that Mario didn't know what to make of: "Such a boor you are, López: making the ladies wait for you."

He pushed open the door and Blanca was there, standing next to his drawing table. She looked up at him and came to him as she never had before, as if they were lovers already. She came to him and took his face between her hands to keep him from giving her two little kisses on the cheeks, and she kissed him on the lips, and the taste of her mouth was made all the more delicious to Mario by the pride he felt at being kissed that way in front of his colleagues.

Nine

NOW THE WOMAN who was not Blanca was walking down the hall toward him in Blanca's green silk blouse and tight jeans, moving with a rhythm that wasn't exactly the rhythm of Blanca's footsteps, though she was wearing Blanca's high-heeled shoes, or a pair of identical high-heeled shoes that revealed the delicate arch of her instep. Now when Mario heard her walking through the house, her footsteps resonated differently, in a silence that was denser than even Blanca's worst and most agonized silences, the ones that all Mario's most devoted and submissive tenderness hadn't been able to break through. But now the silence was different. He'd gotten into the habit of differentiating it with the same mental and sensory acuity that had enabled him to perceive that the woman who lived with him and dressed and spoke like Blanca was not Blanca, however perfectly she was trying to impersonate her, and that Blanca had left him, just as he'd always feared.

He wasn't crazy, but there was no one he could talk to about his very serious suspicion that the woman he lived with was no longer Blanca, and this plunged him into the morbid solitude of someone who possesses an unconfessable secret. Any friend he might mention it to would undoubtedly find the suspicion completely outlandish, and he also came to realize, only now, that during the years he'd spent with Blanca he'd lost all his friends, who had generally struck Blanca as boring or lowbrow, and whom he, with cowardly submissiveness, hadn't had the courage to keep up with, just as he hadn't preserved his former habits or personal tastes—and all so he could pretend to be someone he wasn't, pretend to be on the same level as a woman who could never love him, even if she'd once tried to with a certain degree of conviction. A few days before she left, when Mario saw it all before him as clearly and irreparably as if it had already happened, he went to see her at the Savings and Loan and in a perfectly calm and natural tone of voice asked Blanca what on earth she saw in Onésimo, that obvious phony who had undoubtedly spotted her as easy prey and who described the heaps of bricks and piles of cables that under his tyrannical direction had been strewn here and there across the gallery, accompanied by explanatory wall texts in Valenciano and English, as "works of art."

"My poor little darling, I can't expect you to be able to understand," Blanca said, standing there in front of Mario, and she gave him a quick caress that was undeniably condescending, even pitying, but that paralyzed him with tenderness. "Being with Lluís is like standing at the edge of a cliff with Laurence Olivier in *Rebecca*.... You're like my home. It's as if you and I were sitting on a park bench together, like a couple in an old photograph. That's the difference."

During the good times, she'd been thankful for the steadiness of his character, the serene stability she herself lacked and that had helped her so much to emerge from the deep pit she was in when they met. "You hold me up," she used to say. "You're my foundation in the earth."

Now the calm strength she'd once valued had been turned against him. She no longer wanted the home he had given her or the peaceful life he had woven around and for her, to defend her, as she herself used to say, from the worst part of her soul. Now she was making comparisons to movies and citing passages from works of literature. She wanted to peer down into the abyss, as if she knew what that word really meant, as if she hadn't always been able to count, ultimately, on the protection of her family's money and the solidity of her class.

Standing there in the gallery facing Blanca—Onésimo had granted her the greatest joy of her life by choosing her to be the show's guard, for he claimed that the border between art and life had ruptured and in his installations there was no distance between the guard and the artist or between the guide and the public—Mario understood that he had lost everything, although at that moment he couldn't quite remember the movie Blanca had alluded to; from its name he knew it had to be one of those subtitled black-and-white movies that played on TV late at night. So often, when he told her it was time to go to bed, Blanca would say no, she wanted to watch some Japanese or French movie with subtitles, and he'd go to bed and calculate in the darkness the number of days it had been since they went to bed at the same time, and he'd fall asleep hearing as if from very far away, from the other side of the stucco partition that separated the bedroom from the living room, the soundtrack of the movie she was watching with a fervor she almost never manifested toward real things, the words spoken in a language he didn't understand but in which she could repeat long citations for her friends.

He survived successive phases of fatalism and resolve, faked courage and irremediable desolation. Very often now when he got home at 3:05 or 3:10, Blanca wasn't waiting for him; according to her she was held up at the gallery by her work that wasn't simply, she stressed, in words borrowed from Onésimo, the work of a passive guard or mere repressive delegate of the authoritarian eye. Still, when she wasn't going to be home in time for lunch, she would leave Mario a note, written in the private-school handwriting he liked so much, and she always tried to leave some food for him that he only needed to heat up. At those moments, Mario's guilt would diminish or sweep away his fear, and he'd spend all afternoon waiting for Blanca, or screw up his courage and go to meet her at the Savings and Loan cultural center, overcoming not only his repugnance at the thought of running into Onésimo but also something else he had a very hard time confessing to himself: the shooting stab of shame he felt for her when he heard the ridiculous pedantry of the things Blanca would say as she repeated expressions in French or English that Onésimo had once used or cited in some interview.

She was a different Blanca, and only he, her husband, was aware of her charade, the agitated state of her nerves, the imperceptible flush that rose into her face whenever Onésimo praised her. One day as he watched her in silence from across a table full of people talking loudly and smoking, all presided over by the artist from Valencia, he thought, "If you loved me, I'd make sure you never lost your self-respect."

Ten

THAT LUNCH WAS the end of everything, Mario remembered later when he tried to establish all the details in his mind, pursuing even the slightest tangible clue to Blanca's escape and the appearance of this strange woman in his home. The lunch was held in honor of the closing of the exhibit or installation or whatever it was that had made the cultural center of the Savings and Loan look like a construction site for a month, and was attended by artists, literary people, local journalists, and the director of the bank's Cultural Division, who, perhaps the better to represent the institution that was paying for the meal, felt entitled to order a monstrous lobster which he proceeded to make short work of at almost the same velocity and sound volume at which Lluís Onésimo was ingesting his own lunch.

Alone and quiet, sitting across from Blanca, who was drinking far too much wine and paying rapt attention to Onésimo's words but none at all to his loud mastication, Mario had to fight back a desire to burst into tears or stand up and leave, telling himself that his self-respect was still intact, or at least his patience, and that the following day, after Onésimo was gone, he could embark once more on the task, now so habitual and beloved, of winning Blanca back through the simple, unconditional force of his love. But he also vaguely, painfully intuited that he might no longer have the energy to go on loving her and go on enduring lunches like this one, listening to all the intellectual terminology he didn't understand, all the complicated names of foreign dishes and varieties of wines that now aroused a raging secret hostility in him that only with considerable effort could he keep from extending to Blanca, as well.

The next day, after an extremely unpleasant misunderstanding that cost him almost an hour in Personnel, he got home at about 3:30, still annoyed and also worried that Blanca might have been sitting there waiting for him all that time with the food growing cold. He opened the door and didn't hear Blanca's footsteps in the hallway or music from the TV, and when he reached the living room the evidence that she wasn't there, that she hadn't left him any food, and hadn't even bothered to put the cloth on the table as she always did, fell on him like a blow to the back of the neck. In the small living room of his middle-income housing apartment, surrounded by his own familiar furniture, in front of the blank TV screen where he saw his silhouette reflected, Mario López felt that his world was coming to an end. The definitive, silent cataclysm he had so often imagined and foreseen had arrived, nevertheless, with the horrible force of something absolutely novel. To have been left by Blanca was to sit there staring like an idiot at the crocheted doily that she hated, listening for no reason to someone's footsteps or voice in the apartment upstairs, and feeling that all these things together constituted the devastating totality of his misfortune.

He discovered that some of Blanca's clothes and her small black suitcase were missing from the bedroom's built-in closet. He wanted to believe she'd had to go away for some urgent reason: her mother had suddenly fallen ill or she'd been summoned to an interview for one of the jobs she was always trying to get and then quitting.

Mario went to the kitchen and poured himself a beer. As he cut a slice of mortadella, he noticed he was leaning lower over the edge of the table than he normally did and an instant later he was sobbing violently. To live not only the rest of his life but even that whole afternoon or just the next five or ten minutes seemed an impossible feat he would never be able to achieve. He managed to get hold of himself and went into the studio, seeking further evidence of Blanca's flight. The little radio Blanca spent many afternoons listening to classical music on was no longer in its place on the shelf. In a fit of rage that brought him some fleeting relief, a childish sense of revenge, Mario ripped the poster for Lluís Onésimo's exhibit from the wall. A crumpled sheet of paper in the wastebasket made his heart leap. When he smoothed it out, he saw that Blanca had written "Dear Mario" on it, but hadn't gone on, perhaps, he thought, out of fear of being distracted from her goal, or fear that he would walk in on her just as she was leaving him.

He summoned the courage to call the Savings and Loan gallery and ask for Onésimo. The receptionist, who knew Mario, told him Onésimo had gone back to Madrid on the 2:30 Talgo train, the same hateful express train Blanca was always wanting to take: it was her connection to the exhibits at the Reina Sofía museum, the round tables at the residencia de estudiantes, the French movies at Alphaville, and all the other things she was so enthusiastic about, all the other things that excluded Mario.

He hung up the phone without daring to ask the receptionist whether she happened to have seen Blanca that day. Then he collapsed onto the sofa, his face buried in a pillow, and lay there crying and groping for a box of Kleenex to blow his nose with. He noticed, vaguely, that the light was changing; night was falling.

He awoke in darkness, hearing a key in the door and seeing the hallway light come on. The woman he did not yet know was not Blanca came toward the dining room with footsteps so like Blanca's that at first Mario thought it really was Blanca. Moreover, in the dim light of the dining room, her hair seemed the same, the shape of her face, the brief rosy smile on her sensual lips that still, to Mario's delight, retained a slightly swollen look, like a child's. She looked a bit tired as she walked toward him, though she was smiling as if nothing had happened. She asked what on earth he was doing lying there in the dark, and it took him a while to react, partly because crying and sleeping had had an anesthetic effect on his mind. He got up and took her in his arms, and as he clung tightly to her long, supple body (she was taller than he was, even when she wore flat shoes), his eyes filled with tears again and he thought, with profound emotion and involuntary literary allusion, that he forgave her everything and wouldn't ask her a single question or voice a single reproach.

Then out of the corner of his eye he noticed the first clue: he wasn't sure the bag Blanca had brought home was the same one that was missing from their closet. But it isn't easy to tell one piece of luggage from another; everyone is always mistaking their bag for someone else's at airport luggage claims. Blanca kissed him on the mouth, leaning down a little and separating her lips a millimeter more than usual, and Mario noticed, or later remembered having noticed, that there was no trace of nicotine or red wine on her breath and her hair didn't smell exactly the same.

But he couldn't always be alert and on guard, scrutinizing the woman who little by little was not Blanca, who grew more unfamiliar to the precise degree that she achieved a more perfect likeness, while the other Blanca, the real Blanca, his Blanca, must be living the life she'd always wanted to live, in Madrid or in Valencia, the life that Mario, according to her, had kept her from.

He was giving in. He knew that he was letting himself be swept along by circumstances; the inert, accommodating side of himself that Blanca had never accepted was gently, almost tenderly pushing him to accept the impostor's presence. He washed the dishes in the kitchen after dinner and heard her coming down the hall, her way of walking identical to Blanca's, and when the footsteps stopped he didn't turn around or raise his head from the sink; he knew that the woman who was not Blanca was standing in the doorway, leaning against the doorframe in a posture of laziness or relaxed camaraderie that the real Blanca would never have adopted.

He looked long into her eyes before kissing her and she burst out laughing and told him not to look at her like that: the force of Mario's gaze scared her, and this constituted further and definitive proof of her imposture, because Blanca, his wife, the woman he had loved, the woman who had undoubtedly left him for someone else, had never given any indication that his eyes made a strong impression on her.

He tried to catch her out. He'd call from the office and then stay very silent and listen to her voice, trying to detect an inflection or accent that didn't sound like Blanca. The radio was back in its usual spot on a bookshelf in the room Blanca no longer called the studio, but Mario could have sworn that the radio, too, though very similar, was not the same, and he despaired retrospectively over the scant attention he'd paid to such things, in the provincial haze, the lover's daze he'd lived in until then. In any case, Blanca hardly ever listened to classical music anymore and never locked herself in the studio.

And yet, despite all his snooping around and fits of obsession, and without really noticing it, Mario was less and less unhappy. A night came when he accepted that Blanca wasn't coming back and that it didn't really bother him so much anymore to live with this other woman who looked so much like her. He was lying in his bedroom, doing a little reading, or trying to anyway, because he never relaxed his vigilance, and the door opened and the woman who was not Blanca came in, closing it slowly behind her, and lay down next to him, looking at him with those eyes that were not Blanca's eyes, and unlike Blanca she didn't ask him to turn off the light, and he could take full pleasure in every detail of Blanca's naked body, those he knew by heart and those that surprised or disconcerted him, he wasn't sure whether it was because they belonged to another woman or because he'd never noticed them before.

Then, turning on his side to bring her closer, so close that he breathed in her breath and saw his own anxious, masculine face in her pupils, he closed his eyes and squeezed them tightly shut, afraid that if he opened them the illusion would dissolve, because now he was sure, his eyes shut and wet with tears, that the woman who was holding him was not Blanca: Blanca would never have breathed heavily and moaned like that, Blanca, the other one, the real one, the almost identical one, the one it no longer bothered him to have lost, the one he was not going to see if he opened his eyes, would never have burst out laughing in his arms or murmured in his ear the sweet, shameless words this unknown woman was whispering to him.